THE RIVER IS THE BORDER
From Eritrea to Freedom

Ghirmay Neghasi
and
Iris Sandkuhler

" Leaving your home Country is not a choice"

I am the Voice for the Voiceless !

04/2/2022

This novel is a work of (historical) fiction. The events, locales, characters, names, and conversations are loosely based on the memories of the co-author, as well as a conglomeration of the stories and experiences of other asylum seekers whom he encountered during his journey from Eritrea to the United States.

For discussions and insight, we invite you to visit our
Facebook page. Search the title: The River is the Border, a
Book by Ghirmay Neghasi and Iris Sandkuhler

For a more immersive experience, enter the geographical
locations (mentioned at the beginning of each chapter) into
Google Earth and "fly" along the routes described in this novel.

INTRODUCTION

THE DINNER PARTY
The interview for this book begins at 10:10 a.m., April 25, 2012, at the Strawberry Starbucks in Mill Valley, California.

When Robel said goodbye to his family in Eritrea, Africa, at the age of 18, he was one of many children picked up at his high school by buses transporting the emergency draftees to secret, hidden desert boot camps. He never returned.

Robel and I worked at Starbucks around April 2008. I'd needed a filler (artist survival) job to make my independent-contractor-art-teacher-artist-&-writer ends meet. I've been a coffee addict since I was 12 years old, so I figured it might be fun immersing myself in coffee culture while making a little extra money. For Robel, it was his first employment in the United States and one of the many jobs he needed to get established, earn income, and become a citizen. When we worked the same shifts, I would prompt him to tell me stories about his country Eritrea and how he'd ended up in a small coffee shop in Marin County, California.

A young, gentle face and small, lean, stature belied his 26 years, and was in stark contrast to the harrowing snippets he told me while making lattes and mopping the floor. At times, I started to suspect he was making it all up. His journey sounded more like an epic novel than true-to-life facts. Each "page" of his story made me crave more, but rather in a continuous narrative, uninterrupted by the hectic, high-volume, early morning rush for caffeine. I decided to invite him over for dinner and discovered that he'd only been in the United States for around five months.

That evening, he told me stories that stretched the dinner party from a couple of hours, to late into the night. The dinner version included more details, plus the stories of other travelers (woven in), whose journeys paralleled his in so many ways.

The evening culminated with the two of us sitting comfortably in front of my large computer screen. I was obsessed with (then new) Google Earth. His face lit up as we managed to find and zoom in on his family's home in Eritrea. We *flew* through the landscape of his youth and set off to retrace his trek across the Sahara Desert towards guaranteed indefinite asylum. I was astounded and disturbed by the geographical obstacles that he had overcome. In a moment of exuberance and carelessness, I threw out, "I should write a book about you!"

After leaving Starbucks, I *did* write a book, but it wasn't about Robel. I was contacted by Schiffer Publishing, who had stumbled upon my metalsmithing, teaching website. They asked me to write a book, and my full attention went into that for a good year.

Robel and I continued to visit our local coffee shop even after we'd moved on to other jobs and career pursuits. We would often run into each other, hug, and quickly catch up on life over coffee. Each time he saw me, he asked if I was ready to write his book. I always had an excuse: too busy, packed schedule, travel teaching, moving my elderly mother in, endless deadlines and distractions, etc.

The day came when the timing was perfect. I had just lost "my driver's side girl" to breast cancer and, although I had a clean bill of health, life had taken on a sense of urgency. I was also exhausted, thinking about my mortality. The idea of capturing and weaving his stories filled me with the same sense of excitement and escape that picking up an exotic, juicy, thick novel provided. I was ready.

I asked Robel why he wanted to document his journey. *Posterity,* he replied, in so many words—to share it with his children. He also wanted to show how people struggle for a better life and mostly ... to stay free. His quest towards freedom began in 2001.

AFRICA

ERITREA

MINI TRAINING CAMP
Location: Mendefera and Gahatelay, Eritrea
Interview: 9:35 a.m., May 10, 2012, Strawberry Starbucks, Mill
Valley, CA

Waiting for Robel at the Strawberry Starbucks on May 10, 2012, I studied the furiously scribbled notes in my journal while sipping coffee. Robel had canceled his last appointment with me because he was at the hospital taking care of his son, age 12, who came down with malaria again.

I'd mentioned that I planned to give him the printed draft at some point so he could double check that I'd gotten all of the facts right. The panicked look in his eyes confused me until he suggested maybe we could read our book, out loud, together.

When I worked with Robel only a few years ago, at the same Starbucks, it was difficult to understand him through his thick accent, limited vocabulary, and confusion of past and present tense. Maybe his reading comprehension hadn't caught up enough yet to present him with our book and expect him to proofread it? I reminded myself that proofreading the book was a long time down the road.

My head is filled with impressions of the 18-year-old Robel going off to a makeshift boot camp, then war, in the desert. He is telling me his story, and I'm still not sure how I want to write about it. What angle? Interview? Dictation? Narrative? Simultaneously paralleled with my journal and impressions? Accompanied with maps? Illustrations? Photography? What would I photograph? Interactive Google Earth?—And how do I integrate the subplots of the other people he met along the way? How do I keep everyone anonymous?

I tried using my iPhone to record and translate his voice into written words, but his thick accent just confused the program. He laughed when I asked him if he had any photos from his childhood or journey that I might include. No, of course not.

Right now, I just have to get these notes into some sort of word processing program so that I can begin editing and organizing the chapters and stories.

Here goes …

Mendefera is Robel's hometown. Robel's nearby high school was peopled with students of a variety of ages: from 16 all the way up to 30 years old. Not everyone had the same opportunity to begin school at the same age. There wasn't any shame in getting an education later in life.

Robel came from a middle-class family. His father was a trader [wholesaler] who owned men's and women's boutiques in Mendefera. He would travel to the Port of Massawa to pick up his goods. His mother stayed at home to take care of the five boys and three girls. The children would help out at the shops. They had a happy family life.

At the time of this writing, his parents are still alive and residing in Mendefera. When he turned 18, it was his turn to participate in the emergency draft to prepare for the border war with Ethiopia. It was announced at his school, right before it was completely shut down because, according to Robel, Ethiopia had attacked two schools in other cities.

The young draftees and their suitcases were gathered into buses and driven to a base camp approximately 93 away, roughly near the town of Gahatelay. There were about 40 young men per bus and, since they were picked up regionally, many knew each other. It took around five or six hours of driving in temperatures of 110 degrees Fahrenheit to reach their destination. The duration of boot camp should have been six months but, because of the urgency of the war, they were trained in just two.

Were the young men full of testosterone-driven excitement? Were some afraid? Robel said *yes* to both and added that some of the boys were looking forward to leaving school.

A typical day at their secret military training camp began at five or six in the morning, before the landscape turned into a blast furnace. After morning drills came a breakfast of wheat bread and tea. Lunch and dinner were lentil soup and more bread. The draftees rested for three to four hours, then resumed training from about 4:00-6:00 p.m. Dinner was around 7:00 p.m. The mid-day rest period (11:00 a.m.-3:00 p.m.) was mostly spent in a tent under the trees because it was too hot to move. Robel would read, listen to a radio, or hand-wash clothes. Tanker trucks hauled water in. Had to go to the bathroom? No latrine. You just found a spot behind a bush, out in the desert somewhere. Their basic diet lacked fruit, meat, or vegetables. Since none of the parents knew where their children were, it was not possible to send the troops care packages.

What was the mood of the draftees? Robel's voice was animated as he struggled in broken English to express the feeling of an 18-year-old's resignation.

> If you late training, for even … one … minute ... they make you sit in HOT sun.

> Or make you run hills and back as punish. Or [he imitates marching with his arms and pivoting torso] on hard, hot, ground on [bare] knees. If you refuse [he scowls] they make you … THEY MAKE YOU. Whatever your excuse, they don't listen ...

I asked Robel to tell me the three worst things about his stint in boot camp.

> If you don't feel good, it don't matter. They don't care. If you sick, there's not hospital. Not medicine near … training camp. *Maybe* if you sick for *two* or *three* weeks, they take you military hospital. Maayyybeeee. We don't know when it end. We always think: Today we go battle? Tomorrow? When?

It was clear to Robel that their lives were expendable.

Perhaps a tougher question was: *If* you had to find something good about the experience, what would it be? He said that meeting other people from all corners of his country was interesting. Some of his best friends from high school were there, and they'd grown up in the same area.

What was his mental attitude at that point?

> Go with it. Get through it. Because you don't have ... no choice. No option. Make yourself *strong* [his brow furrows as he makes a fist pump in the air] survive battle at the border ... Ya.

Each day, the person in charge would count the draftees. If someone disappeared, there were a lot of assumptions. Did they run away to the border? Did they die in the hot, dry landscape from abuse, neglect, or punishment? No one in charge cared.

The desert-camouflaged zip-up tents were hidden under trees so that the helicopters couldn't spot them. There weren't any civilians living close by, but according to Robel, *there were plenty of snakes and scorpions to keep you company.* Sometimes the nights were so hot that the soldiers had to move their tents out into a dry wash, in the open, to get more air. When the horn blew at 5:00 a.m., everyone picked up their tents and carried them to the forest, to hide under the trees.

BATTLE FOR THE BORDER
Location: Senafe & May Ayni, Eritrea

When Robel's time came to get shipped out, he estimates there were about 1500 people (500 per battalion) in his boot camp. Approximately 120 of them were separated and assigned to different locations along the southern border of Eritrea and Ethiopia.

Three open trucks picked up the high-school youths, each carrying a full military pack. In it, Robel had a cup, bowl and spoon, sugar, powdered milk, crackers, biscotti (Italian colonization influence), a protein drink (powdered barley that you shake up with water and powdered milk), tennis shoes, underwear, and T-shirts. He also carried a Kalashnikov rifle. On his belt, he had three Russian and two Chinese grenades, two knives, and a canteen. He wore a ball cap-style military hat. What Robel didn't have (and was surprised at my asking) was a map or filtration system for water, since they collected water wherever and whenever. Of course, in my limited experience, while listening to his story, I'm thinking *camping*, not poverty, under preparedness and battle. Their gear also did not include sunglasses, bathroom shovel, or toilet paper. Lotion for sun protection was unheard of and made him chuckle at the idea of it.

It took one day and a half to reach the first camp, on the southern border, where everyone was further subdivided into roughly 50 stations. One camp managed approximately 93 miles of terrain that was mostly flat, sandy desert with occasional sand dunes. You could see mountains about 10 miles away. No roads.

Senafe, located in southern Eritrea, on the edge of the Ethiopian highlands, was the closest town to where Robel was assigned to live for five months. No battles were fought there. The soldiers dug trenches to hide in and built underground tunnels, cleaned their weapons, and rotated sentry duty. His responsibilities included cutting trees in the forest for kitchen wood.

After five months, he was assigned (along with others) to switch with a crew that was on the firing line, and he needed rest. It was roughly 50 miles closer to the Ethiopian border near the town of May Ayni, Eritrea. Robel arrived at night when things were quiet, but the next day, the shooting resumed on the battlefield. The Ethiopian soldiers advanced down the valley on foot, in tanks and trucks–through the forest and on the road. Robel and his comrades hid in the hills behind rocks for cover. Attacks came from the ground, so they didn't have to worry about air raids. The soldiers were rotated out every five hours to take a break. A 20-year-old runner was assigned to deliver ammunition so that no one had to leave their combat posts.

During Robel's first day of battle, the Ethiopians were driven out of the valley, but on the second day they returned. On the third day, Robel found himself out of ammunition, and the runner wasn't available. After waiting quite some time, he made the decision to crawl back to where it was stored and get it himself. It was during this attempt that he was hit and wounded in both legs. "Bullets or shrapnel?" I asked. He didn't know.

They loaded him onto a stretcher, then into a truck and drove some 20 miles away from the border to receive first aid. From there, he was transferred to a hospital because of excessive bleeding. No X-rays were taken, and no exit wounds were found in his lean body, but the damage was severe enough that Robel spent six weeks in the hospital. He couldn't walk and spent most of his time resting and going to physical therapy. The food was a step up in quality, nutrition, and variety. He had meat, vegetables, and lots of Italian dishes including pasta. Mostly, he told me, he was grateful that his life had been spared. This was, however, tempered with anxiety about what would come next.

THE FARM IN ALIGIDER
Location: Near Teseney, in the Gash-Barka Region of Eritrea

Once Robel recovered from his wounds and was finished with rehabilitation, the military sent him to rejoin his crew, which at that point, was stationed in southwestern Eritrea, approximately 28 miles from the Sudanese border.

The terrain around the market town of Teseney was mostly rough and flat with mountains abruptly jutting out of a tanned landscape. The Gash river provided water, and its banks were green with native vegetation-- mostly shrubbery, eucalyptus, aloes, and cacti.

Far from the war, the bucolic, irrigated landscape lent itself to farming cotton, sorghum and sesame. Robel found himself on a huge farm near the market town of Teseney in a place called Aligider, where his crew had been sent to rest from their tour on the battlefield. Everyone was under the impression that it was a government-owned farm.

Each day on the farm, Robel would exercise, continue his military training, and then work the fields in temperatures well over 100 degrees Fahrenheit. The generals, who lived in a nearby town, visited two or three days a week to see how things were progressing. Punishments were dispensed regularly to encourage the troops to work harder and faster in the fields. As for boot camp, there wasn't any sympathy for anyone who became ill or didn't cooperate.

The barn and main house reflected Italian architecture. There were a dozen people assigned to each workers' cottage. Despite being a farm, the food wasn't very exciting: lettuce, soup, bread, coffee, and tea. But their meals did include meat once a week on Sundays, usually goat or lamb.

I asked Robel what a typical day was like on the farm.

The schedule fluctuated according to the farm's needs. He said he would get up at six in the morning and work clearing weeds, building and maintaining irrigation, digging water trenches, planting seeds, picking cotton, and carrying it in sacks to the trucks. Several civilian women managed meals, with breakfast from 11:00 a.m. until noon. Noon began free time, and Robel mostly napped. At 12:30 p.m. until 1:30 p.m. or 2:00 p.m., the soldiers were organized in military formation and would run up to 20 miles for exercise. From 2:00 pm until 3:00, they ate lunch. Four through 6:00 p.m. was dinner, followed by free time. On Saturdays, there wasn't any military training. Sundays were a day of rest.

"Was there ever an opportunity to get off the farm and explore the area?" I questioned. The nearest town was a two-hour walk, so, no—unless you could hitch a ride. Once, Robel did just that, with dire consequences.

> Sunday morning is Day of the Rest and you can go anywhere as long as you back. Then I want one day, I want to city Teseney, ya at ... to see my family members living city, and I want, you know, red truck, to deliver bread us from town of Teseney, to go back to city. Ya.
>
> And then when I go there ... family members, we lunch, together. Then cousin from family member hanging out too, at bar. Like alcohol bar. We keep drinking. I, we get drunk, so I missed truck back camp. So I spending night at family member house. As ... ya, since I am drunk, I am late missing Monday work farm.
>
> Then when I go back to, uh ... my place ya, my-uh what do you call person you call *lead* [officer?], call me what happen. I am available to work? And I say him story and he say "it's your responsibility, you know, you be here Monday start time." Then I tell him, I lost [missed] truck I come back. Don't say him I was ... alcohol

[drunk]. And he say "Go get off all your civil clothes, wear your uniform. Come back." I wearing my regularly old clothes. Changed into military clothes and back to leader and he say lend [lay] on floor [ground]. Spread all milled [milk] on top me. Tied my hands behind back on ground. Face down. Then you have to ... mud water, mud very water, flipped down. Turned over three four times. All dirty and milled. All ants drop on you. Stay at least one hour. Mud. Once they see you all dirty then you can stay there, with mud, milled, clothes, everythings. Ants all over your body and they keep checking you. Every 10 minutes. Then, oh ... horrible. Very bad. They bite, bite, *bite,* chew!

Robel thrashes his head back and forth at our table (and the coffee sloshes out of our cups) to illustrate getting imaginary ants off his face. While Robel continues to dictate his torture story, a coffee drinker at the next table looks at us quizzically.

Robel lowered his voice and hissed, "... rest of you ok, but especially your face. "

After one hour they came and say me, untie me, "You get up." Not even hour and half you have washing all your clothes. Get dry. Straight up and clean! Wear uniform. Come back. Keep wash dry. Wearing all clothes and then I go back. They say me, "Do you know why?" Ya I know. If I say no, it be worse. Mayybeee worse. [He chuckles.] I just say them ya. I miss a day and go. Don't ask permission. Ya ... Yes ... why next time ... be more punish. I never do again. Have bite marks all over face. [He inflates his cheeks.]

Swollen? I ask.

Ya. Swollen. Friends laughing you. You stay quiet. You do *know* you will get punish. It's not just me. It's lot people ... get punish. You respect you get hard punish. No choice.

After working in harsh conditions for three to four months, they discovered that the property was privately owned by three generals, with one of them specifically in charge. A first cousin, of one of these generals, was part of the work crew. He divulged the secret one day: the generals were business partners and had manipulated the military to use the soldiers for free labor. The government was not keeping a close watch and thought the troops were just recovering from battle and training to stay sharp, on a farm.

FREE FARM LABOR
Location: Aligider, Eritrea
Interview: 8:45 a.m., July 23, 2012, Strawberry Starbucks, Mill Valley, CA

Once the truth came out, resentment grew amongst the troops, and 25 soldiers decided to strike. They announced to their supervisor that they refused to work for private profiteering any longer.

Sitting across from a 30-year-old Robel, I probed deeper to try and get some insight into his 20-year-old soldier's mind. A young mind that had only participated in an abbreviated two years of Eritrean military experience when all this occurred. Why would he risk a strike?

He explained: "Farm work two, three hours in day, but what's point? We not farming food for government. They just use you like a ... uh ... throw away. Ya throw cup. No future." Robel swept the air with his hands to paint a picture of the impossible daily goals "You must complete this many [acres] in this time or you punish." He takes the edge of one hand and hits his flat palm, chop, chop, chop.

The work stoppage news went up the command chain, but nothing happened. Not right away. No one came to question the soldiers about their decision. When Robel and his comrades were not engaged in military drills, they spent their time praying, reading books, and hanging out. Because they congregated in a large, empty cottage to pray, the supervising soldiers suspected they were plotting against them. After approximately a week of this new routine, one of the generals showed up for a visit and had a supervisor brief him on the situation. They observed the young men gathering regularly in the cottage, in what appeared to be meetings. The general left.

15

A week later, the general returned and collected 10-armed soldiers from the farm to accompany him. One by one, Robel and his comrades were ordered out of the wooden, thatched cottage and made to sit against its outer wall. What happened? They were interrogated. Why had they refused to work? Robel was the first to respond to the question. His high-school friends Merhawi and Meseret chimed in. The rest of the group remained passively silent. After the interview, they were all told to return to their shared rooms and never to gather as a group again.

Relieved, the rest of the day unfolded without incident. They ate dinner and went to bed at the usual hour. Around midnight, Robel, Merhawi, and Meseret were abruptly woken up by armed soldiers. Merhawi was taken to a military canvas-covered truck first. It had pulled up right next to the cottage. When Robel answered the knock on his door, they told him to wake Meseret. They had seconds to gather their personal items and were ordered to leave their weapons behind.

"We shocked," Robel emphasized, "…when we see Merhawi sitting inside truck [guarded by] two soldiers."

As they lurched off, Robel observed that the general, accompanied by a soldier, was sitting in the cab. Robel and his friends didn't know where they were headed during the next five hours. When they asked, the response was "don't talk" and simply "you'll see when you here."

Around six-thirty in the morning, they arrived at a prison, carved into the base of a mountain, in the middle of a forest, located somewhere between Sawa and Haykota. It was "really big," Robel's eyes widened as he remembered. The compound included roughly 80 prisoners as well as some offices, staff, weapons, and food storage. I asked Robel if he could make a simple drawing for me so that I could understand the layout better. It looked confusing on the paper napkin, but one thing stood out: There would be no escape from the compound.

Curious, I researched Eritrean prisons on the Internet and tried to pinpoint possible locations on Google Earth. Perhaps others have written about their experiences. Could I find his? With our global connectivity and the Human Rights Campaign, there may even be photos available now.

What I discovered were references to so many prisons that it was shocking and exhaustive. The next time we met, I showed him the alphabetized list of prisons compiled from three web sites: www.assenna.com, www.ehrea.org, and awate.com/

Some of the 37 entries included brief descriptions of various prision "constructions" such as police stations, underground cells, shipping containers, military detention centers, barracks, and sheet metal buildings. It was noted, that with most, there was little or no ventilation, no temperature controls (the weather could swing wildly from extreme heat to frigid cold) and with no oppotunity to wash, use actual toilet facilities, or have any sort of medical attention.

Some of the reasons (listed on the websites) for being rounded up (such as at Robel's high shool) and/or arrested included: religious and political beliefs, military punishment, draft dodging, detention, interrogation, illegal border crossings, slave labor, or foiled attempts to escape.

Activities within the prison system included forced labor, solitary confinement, rape, sexual abuse, interrogation, torture, chaining of prisoners, and psychological intimidation. Many of the prisoners were sadistically abused immediatly before getting moved to a different location.

Robel was unable to definitively recognize the prison he was sentenced to. I got the impression that he was overwhelmed by all of the images. Or perhaps, he had blocked it all out.

The list of prisons at awate.com/eritrea-the-network-of-prisons-2/

has links that take you to Google Earth so that you can get an aerial view of the locations. The last time I checked, photos were also included with the maps.

IN PRISON FOR FARM STRIKE
Location: Somewhere between Sawa and Haykota, Eritrea
Interview: 9:52 a.m., July 30, 2012, Strawberry Starbucks, Mill
Valley, CA

Not quite a child soldier, Robel had been drafted into the
emergency army on January 28, 1999. Now it was May 2001,
and he was facing prison in the middle of nowhere. Robel
remembered that day vividly. He was the first in his group to
be interviewed at the prison compound's office. It was about
105 degrees Fahrenheit that day and painfully bone dry.

The prison that Robel found himself in had been blasted and
carved out of the side of a small mountain. The rock-and-
cement interior structure was roughly the size of the Starbucks
that we are sitting in for our weekly morning interview. He
describes the only way out: one guarded door. No provisions
for real air circulation. All the prisoners were sharing the same
dark cell.

The compound was surrounded by 1-1/2 stories high, razor
wire made with blades facing both directions. After sitting in
the dark for two hours, Robel's interview began.

"You know why you here?," asked his interrogator.

"I don't know," he replied passively.

Of course Robel knew, but he also knew that the less
information he gave them to use against him, the better.

The interrogator continued, "He ... [the general] report you
make [instigated] stop working [I introduced him to the word
"strike"] in fields. You [led] more than 25 people. You first
person [organize] them, so *you are their leader*."

Robel replied that he had not organized them but that it was a collective decision. It was only because he had talked in front of the cottage at the farm, and had told the truth about discovering that they were being forced to work as non-military farm labor, that the general pegged *him* as the leader.

The interviewer frowned and asked Robel how he knew that it was a private, for-profit farm labor camp. And why did Robel choose not to turn in the guy who disclosed the "erroneous" information?

"Why say them?," Robel explained to me. "I already jail. Why send someone [else] too?" He knew that either way, he would remain in jail.

"Say it or not, you stay prison until you yes [agree] guilty. So I stay where I know ..."

I describe the saying, "knowing my poison" to him: How in medieval days when people poisoned each other to gain power, it was better to "know one's poison," so that you could secretly keep taking the antidote (or spit it out without anyone knowing) rather than face an unknown poison. It's also a way to describe not doing anything about your situation because the alternative could be worse.

"Ya, I know my poison. It best. It can be worse if I say them anything besides 'we' strike," he concluded with a dismissive hand wave.

"Soldiers standing, ready shoot us, we don't talk much. But inside us Merhawi and I prayed."

At the prison, they interrogated Robel's two friends, and he was relieved that they were all on the same page.

For eight months, life in prison was dull. Daily meals consisted of one liter of water, one cup of tea, and a piece of wheat bread. That was it. Their issued clothes included a pair of long brown polyester pants, a dark, almost black T-shirt, and dark, soft plastic shoes. There was no opportunity for any hygiene to speak of, no place to wash, and no soap. If you wanted, Robel told me, you could try to clean up with water from your rationed water.

Bathroom routines consisted of relieving oneself once per day, surrounded by six military guards with other prisoners waiting in a queue. The "bathroom" consisted of little cul-de-sacs in the rocks, with a few trees.

Before sunset, you would use a stone to clean yourself after a bowel movement, with the same protocol of guards surrounding you. All this took place just outside of the manmade prison cave. Robel described the guards as "just doing job." They weren't particularly mean or abrasive.

The irony about this prison situation is that every Wednesday, they were taken from the prison to a nearby agricultural field to cut mature sorghum. Once again, Robel found himself forced into agricultural labor. There were approximately 16 prison guards to 80 prisoners. They would leave around ten in the morning and work in the crops until noon.

At some point, Merhawi, Meseret and Robel decided they'd had enough and wanted to run away. "We tired," Robel said. "We gotta do something."

"So we [he made a huddled motion with his arms over our coffee table] talking low. Inside prison ... because we know next day we work fields. We run away next day. We friends. We decide. We agree. It be worse—they catching us, or it maayyybeeee better—we make it. Time is coming to ... ya, do something!"

Some of the sorghum was the same height as Robel and his friends, but some was even taller. Thirty minutes after their work began, they decided to escape. Their location was relatively close to the Sudan border -- in the direction of where the sun sets. They had taken care to study their local geography.

Robel took off first, running on his hands and knees "like a dog" between the crop rows. The edge of the field was forested. His friend Merhawi was right behind him. A guard spotted Meseret and yelled "Stop! Stop!," then began shooting. Another guard joined in the chase.

With blood pumping in their ears, Robel and Merhawi made it to the edge of the sorghum field and then took off in a westerly direction. They ran for a solid four hours without pause, through forests mostly made of pine, olive, eucalyptus and sharp-leafed oak trees. The terrain was flat, sandy, and *very* dry. Fortunately, it was the end of summer, and the temperature was somewhere between 70 and 75 degrees Fahrenheit. They stopped only when they reached a creek. The water looked clean, but how would they know? In their weakened state, they had no choice but to drink and hope for the best. "So thirsty," Robel said.

> We so thirsty … we not care if we sick on water. Thinking on our friend who don't make it. What happen? There is nothing. Nothing to do. We drinking and resting one hour.

> When we walking, we go sun in west. No mountains, flat and sharp trees. By 5:30, we so, so hungry. Sun set maybe 6:30 and cold begin after midnight. Then we see campfire [he made a flurry motion in the air towards the front of the café] … someone making dinner. We follow fire and go straight. What choice we have? We have take risk. We watch them. Quiet. Lots of noise with sheeps, goats, dogs, cows, camels. When we see they Tigre, we 90 percent sure … they okay.

At the time, Eritrea had nine tribes. The Tigre, an ethnic group of nomadic and pastoralist people, live near the borders of Eritrea and Sudan. They are predominantly Muslim but have some Christians among them (referred to as Mensaï by the Eritreans. Robel belongs to the Biher-Tigrinya, which is close in language to the Tigre tribe.

He recognized some of their words. Because there was no strife between the tribes, Robel and his friend felt safe in approaching the nomads for help. When they stepped into the light of the camp, "They so, so shocked!"

> There five men and two womans. I explain we walking west. We hungry. We can pay for food. I have [rolled up] 2,000 *nakfa* in [he shows me the belt-line] my prison pants. When they making us clothes in prison, I have a moment and … ya … used sharp edge of … uh … metal [rebar]. I find … cut [seam] open. My parents give me money when I leave home.

We stop the interview for a moment, as I search the Internet on my tablet to find a photo of rebar to confirm the type of metal he used to open the waistline of the prison pants. It was.

> You not looking at womans too much or men will be anger. Because they Tigre tribe, womans covered in red and white [fabric] with only eyes show. Men dirty, white clothes … [motions a turban around his head]. Womans make hot, smoothed stones, in fire… and make them hot hot hot! Then they put … [dough] on them to make crispy one-, two-[inch] bread. They use water to stick salt on top.

Robel illustrated stacking invisible loaves with his hands in the air.

> It very, very good. They, uh … milled [milk] boiled in big dish. We get metal [holds an imaginary pitcher between his palms] hot milled … Ya … drink. I pay 200 nakfa for our food. Food sooo good. We just chillin' with them for while.

Next day they put everythings ... put on camels and maybe go 50 miles. They give us one bottle of water [each]. We go night and go west. We make our way, in dark with hands [he demonstrates putting one hand out in front of his face, and the other crossed over his face to protect his eyes]. Tree sticks sharp and our arms bleeding. You have step careful with feet and feel way so don't fall. Control yourself and not make noise. As we close border Sudan, we know military border guards. So we step quiet, shhhh ... listen ... then more step. No choice. We have take risk. Night hiding us. In three hours we crossing border. How we know? Mountains [Taka, Totil, and Aweitila] show city Kassala. Mountains. Ya, you look for mountains, then no mistake. So when you pass mountains you know you are East Sudan.

We so happy. No more Eritreans. Land full of garden houses [huts] with sleeping Sudanese [his arms gesture wide]. We find big vegetable garden [irrigated agricultural field] at two in morning and sleep in cold. We hiding under orange trees.

SUDAN

FROM THE MOUNTAINS OF KASSALA TO KHARTOUM
Location: Kassala and the Jabra neighborhood in Khartoum, Sudan
Interview: 10:10 a.m., August 6, 2012, Strawberry Starbucks, Mill Valley, CA

Waking up, illuminated by daylight, they saw that their arms were covered in scratches and dried blood from making their blind way through the sharp semi-desert landscape the night before. Robel and Merhawi continued through orange groves, then vegetable fields. Eventually they found a road.

"Land, ya, flat, and we see city of Kassala," he said conversationally while sipping his coffee and motioning his hand into a remembered distance, "but it too far walking in desert."

Eventually and predictably, Sudanese soldiers stopped them on the road and asked to see their passports. Of course they had nothing except the clothes on their back and a single water bottle each that the nomads had given them, plus Robel's hidden money rolled and stuffed into the seam of his pants waistline.

The soldiers spoke Arabic, but Robel and Merhawi did not. The situation was obvious to everyone. They climbed into the truck and drove to Kassala's immigration office. "They keeping us in room for two, three days. They understand. We not the first ones. There much ... refugees crossing [sneaking] border."

At the time, Kassala was the main thoroughfare for refugees. Its condensed mountain range abruptly juts out of a largely flat and barren landscape. The group of mountains is so distinct, that it serves as a significant landmark that can be spotted from great distances away.

"We happy having food again: tea, bread and uh … beans for breakfast. Lunch we eat meat on kebab. Dinner we eat pita bread, lentils, sometimes more meat. Sometimes sandwich. Merhawi and I [shared] a … " Robel describes a jail cell and sleeping cots handmade from wood with tightly woven tree fibers stretched across the frame. On top of the thatch were mats, then sheets. It was good to sleep in a bed again.

The immigration center brought in a translator who learned how the soldiers in Robel's unit were forced to do farm labor for profiteering, and how Merhawi and Robel were arrested. They also went over their escape from prison and how running into the Tigre nomads was a small miracle. So many people had been thrown into prison for similar reasons. The Sudanese immigration officer was sympathetic and was just waiting for the general to give permission and let them go.

With time on their hands, Merhawi and Robel walked around a lot and sat in the hot, open-air yard, as well as in their cell. Besides good food, they also enjoyed a real bathroom with running water.

On the third day, they were offered papers to present to the local police station and receive an identification permit, verifying that they could live and work locally. Neither Merhawi nor Robel had any intention of remaining in Kassala. But leaving and surviving would cost more money than Robel had, so he called his father's brother in Khartoum, who lived a nine-hour drive away, to explain the situation. Arefine was shocked at hearing his nephew's voice and asked how he could assist them. It was a matter of money, followed by transport, to join his uncle in the capital of Sudan.

Uncle Arefine had a friend in Kassala to whom he wired the money. Robel didn't want to take a public bus to Khartoum, because every couple hundred miles, there would be a checkpoint. Since the refugees only had permission to live and work locally, they couldn't risk being discovered. So instead, his uncle arranged transport with a semi-truck driver, who had a regularly scheduled route between the Port of Sudan on the Red Sea, Kassala, and Khartoum. He had three semi tractor-trailers with containers which he managed, so nothing would seem out of the ordinary.

Robel was in contact with his uncle via a public phone, and they arranged a meeting place for the transport. Meanwhile, Robel and his friend hid in a hotel because they'd never gone to the police station to get their permits.

After one night, the driver arrived and parked the truck behind a one-story hotel in a dirt lot. The semi had a bed, with curtains, right behind the driver's seat, which provided a great place to burrow into and hide. The truck was comfortably large, new, and best of all, it had air conditioning. It took nine hours to get to Khartoum, and the driver was familiar with all the checkpoints, so they had plenty of time to prepare for each. The checkpoints were more apt to stop buses and search for permits because there were too many official trucks transporting legitimate goods along the major shipping route to be able to stop each one. Robel sat in the passenger seat for most of the journey, and the three of them refreshed themselves at roadside restaurants without problems.

In Khartoum, both Robel and Merhawi spent their first three days at his uncle's home, feeling safe but exhausted. The home had a walled-in back yard with the ground cemented over. Because it was so hot, they would sleep outside at night, on lightweight beds placed under a *gabella* (or in Arabic: *rocuba)*. The structure was made of posts that held up a flat thatched roof. Roomy enough for four small beds, some chairs, plus a television; it also provided shade.

It was a pleasure to shower, watch television and sleep a lot. One morning, Robel couldn't help but sleep through breakfast and didn't get up until nearly noon.

Robel's uncle connected him with his relieved family back home by phone. The family in Eritrea was healthy and safe, but they were all shocked to hear about Robel's misadventures since leaving for the emergency army. His happy parents were also relieved that Robel was no longer in immediate danger.

On the fourth day, Robel's uncle took him to apply and pay for a refugee photo-identification paper at the police station. It cost 300 Junaih. Next, Robel and Merhawi looked for employment and found it in the form of construction work. Some of their daily tasks included digging, mixing cement, hammering and sawing. Robel spoke a little Arabic at this point and helped his best friend Merhawi, who didn't speak any.

After one month, they decided to rent their own little studio-style house. Robel was now 22 years old and Merhawi, 22 or 23 years old. They made a friend at the construction job and soon added him as a third housemate.

ROUTINE LIFE AS A REFUGEE AND CONSTRUCTION
WORKER
Location: Jabra Zone of Khartoum near Block 11, Sudan
Interview: 9:10 a.m., September 3, 2012, Strawberry
Starbucks, Mill Valley, CA

As with any Christian living in a predominantly Muslim area,
there was always an issue. The religious holiday of Ramadan,
for example, provided pressure not to eat if you didn't want to
look conspicuous. But it went beyond that.

> This is how we begin our life in Sudan. It very hot and
> dry. We had drink water all day, construction place.
> Working three or four house, high… Nothing change in
> life. It not a good place life for immigrant and refugee.
> There lots of dis-crim-in-nation. We not look same.
> Police see you and find reason stop you. They ask see
> ID, then check pockets. Keeping what they find, like
> cell phone. Every day. We have be careful police.
> Hiding police. We hiding money walking around.

THE GREAT DESERT CROSSING
Location: Sahara

Merhawi didn't have any financial support, so he couldn't leave Sudan. Robel, on the other hand, had financial support from his parents in Eritrea and uncle in Sudan, which provided a way to leave Sudan. His parents sent $1,000 to Uncle Arefine, who managed the money and eventually helped him to leave. Robel knew a lot of friends who had left Sudan for Libya. He found smugglers who made a living at arranging, bribing, and helping people cross borders illegally. Robel agreed to pay $500 in advance and on good faith, to the brokers to get to Libya. To do so, they would have to cross the great Sahara Desert. The brokers arranged the transportation, water containers, and spare parts for the trucks that would haul the refugees with their minimal belongings. They had to trust their lives to these strangers.

Robel was instructed to prepare dry food, crackers, bottled water, powdered milk (to shake up in bottled water), dried bread, and meat (pulverized jerky) "to add to sauce."

We paused a moment to discuss the dried meat. His uncle bought lamb. It was cut thin and hung upstairs under the roof so that nothing could reach it. "In dry, hot air, don't take long dehy [dehydrate]." Robel used his fist and palm to mimic a mortar and pestle and continued describing the process of breaking it down, "Then you smash it, dig it, dig it, dig it. You know. My uncle … he make this package for me."

A common product for use in desert climates is called ORS, or oral dehydration salts. It's an orange-flavored powder that contains sodium and other ingredients to give you energy and help your body combat extremely hot and dry climates. Everyone brought lots of ORS packets.

The broker said that when all things were in place, he would contact both Robel and the other refugees. They must be ready to depart at a moment's notice. Robel waited uncomfortably, knowing that his money was gone, but in his words, "What else can I do but believe and have faith in God?" Also, the broker wouldn't risk his reputation to steal the money. "It just how things work."

Robel waited a week for the phone call that would change the course of his life in a profound way. Approximately 25 women, 10 children, and 35 men met at night, in a secure house, big enough to hide everyone from the local police. Everyone fiddled nervously with provisions while they waited.

Three open-bed Toyota trucks, with two drivers each, picked them up. "They line you up," Robel said "and squeeze like tomatoes." Cords were used to tie their bags onto the homemade, welded, fence-like barrier edging the truck bed. Everyone held onto it and to each other's shoulders, as the trucks lurched forward and headed northwest.

Robel described their drive towards the desert border as "insane!" They took off under the cover of darkness at 4:00 or 5:00 o'clock in the morning, hitting what felt like every pothole and rut in the road. The refugees wore hats that covered their ears and sunglasses to keep out the dust. Bandanas crossed their faces so they could breathe. Some women wore pants under their dresses, or just pants, shirts, and head wraps.

By daybreak, the truck drivers would sometimes go 100 miles per hour. Conspicuous dust flew upward in tall plumes, marking their intention, for anyone who might be watching and waiting for an opportunity to arrest or attack and rob them. The strategy was simple: Outrun anyone who was even considering chasing them.

They arrived at the edge of the vast Sahara Desert just as the golden sun was going down. Setting up camp, some used their precious cases of water like stools. Others stuffed the new plastic water bottles into their sacks. They ate, drank, and slept nervously.

I asked Robel if he was worried about scorpions seeking out the warmth of his body and nestling underneath him while sleeping on the ground. He said no, he was more worried about dying by the hands of the smugglers who'd taken everyone's money. —or suffocating in quicksand, getting buried by a massive *haboob*, or any number of dangers inherent to crossing a desert of this severity and vastness.

The adults kept a wary eye on the drivers. Will the drivers roar off into the night, leaving everyone stranded? Most of the men carried knives with them in case things went awry.

> *With knife, at least you have pos-si-bility [of getting a]*
> *truck, and your chances … if you are uh … betray.*
> Even if drivers are honest, there are others in desert
> who kill you. Then rob you. For womans it can be worse.

And what about the children? I wondered.

FOR WOMANS, IT COULD BE WORSE
Location: Teseney, Kassala, and unknown
Interview: 9:42 a.m., June 29, 2015, Barnes & Noble, Tiburon, CA

I arrive at Barnes & Noble first, get my coffee and look for a place to plug in my laptop. Usually scoping out a spot away from potential eavesdroppers; this time I'm not so lucky. A young man is reading a magazine in the vicinity. I decide that not losing what I write is more important than someone listening in on our conversation.

Soon Robel arrives, gets in line to buy coffee and glances around. When he sits down with me, he asks about the welfare of each individual in my family, one by one. I remind myself that this is a courteous Eritrean tradition and pace myself slowly to do the same with him.

Before we get down to the business of writing, I notice he is uneasy and stalls. By the expression on his face, I can see that he has come to some sort of conclusion. He suggests, under his breath, that we move. I follow his glance towards the young African nearby.

Once we've settled into a new location in the book shops' café, he clarifies that he has seen the man reading the magazine before, and that he probably wouldn't appreciate Robel revealing the details of his journey across the globe to Marin County. It was best to keep a low profile.

I type as fast as I can on my keyboard to capture the vignette of another young Eritrean as the next story pours out of Robel.

There is story of girl, must be somewhere 'round 16 year old. Ya. She trying crossing border [from Eritrea] to Sudan. She used working in town Teseney, Eritrea, with lady have bar, alcohol. We have home made there. People think … at time there are good jobs in Sudan and lot people, away from enemies, at time get away from them too. Many killed by Ethiopia. Better job and save her life going Sudan.

Then when she got Kassala, and she want a lady's house. Woman, everybody can rested there, and woman been there for long time. Lady, she received them in kind of hotel. And she find job for girl. Girl crossing from Eritrea. Three young girls already got job.

Job is working with family Sudanese man, and be work with them: that verbal. *Real* is she going be with Sudanese man. He come and talking lady, then lady talking to … ya … Eritrean girl been in hotel and they so exited.

And young girl pick up by two men in truck. And after she translate Arabic to her, she is going to come back every week. Lady. They going to send her back one day off to rest house. Visit. So no problem.

Girl excited, she find job. After ya … they come next day, picking her up and she ready go. They came. They driving [towards] east … west of town of Kassala. Maybe two hours driving. In middle of nowhere. In kind of semi-desert.

When she go there, they rape her. And she become his wife. They ... because other men's his friends. She locked in house. Day and night. She don't know where she at. She can't talking anybody. *No one* seeee her. She been there six months. After six months she become baby [pregnant]. Ya, pregnant.

Then when she become pregnant she cannot go anywhere. She started to be going outside. And she go to downtown … little town like a market. Outside market while she walking around 5:30-6:00, she hear radio … radio Tigrinya. And she shocked! And place like *little* restaurant. Sitting lot of chairs outside, 'cause so hot. Tribe they speak Tigre, which is different, but from her language. But when she hear news she speak Tigrinya. She go straight up and say them "I am here, and I have a problem, and you need help me." And they speak a little Tigrinya.

They shocked by story what happen. They say her,"we *can not do anything* now. Everyone see you here. If someone … something happen they gonna come us and maaybee kill us. We need help you in very smart way. Here need to do."

Two days later, they say her, you have to make sure you're ready all your stuff. Then come over here 'round 7:30, become a little dark. They can not see anybody, and those guys have to be ready car."

Take her. And two days later, she go from house to restaurant. They driving her back to Eritrea. Almost 4 ½ hours. They driving.

Girl went back to city Teseney, and they drop her at lady selling homemade drink. Ya, back at lady with bar. She have, I think, uh…eight months pregnant, ya, and lady shocked when she see her. Go for better opportunity and she come back pregnant. She don't know if three young girls have same problem she got.

Once she come back to Eritrea with ... uh, bar lady she used to work, one month to deliver baby. She so stressing out. She depressed. And she always trying say when she deliver, she going throw away baby. Lady she very helpful for her, no worries, it happen. I help you everythings. She give her very good ... positive idea and she helping her everythings she need. But in girl mind, when she deliver, she going throw away. Never keeping baby. After baby deliver, right after [Robel snaps fingers] baby crying. She ... baby touching her heart. So then after she can't do. She can't do it. Then she raised baby. Almost growing. After Eritrea in situation with Ethiopia. She decide ... go back to Sudan, but till this day she don't know who son's father.

That first night, sleeping at the edge of the Sahara, there was a lot of angst for Robel and the refugees around him.

Once the sun came up, they used it and secret landmarks as their guide. It was impossible to drive at night because you would easily get lost, but daytime temperatures could reach a 120 degrees Fahrenheit. The ground temperatures were even higher. "It like oven slowly baking you," said Robel, emphasizing by letting out a tired, long breath.

The smugglers let the air out of the truck tires so that they wouldn't expand and blow out because of heat expansion. It also helped the vehicles grab better in the shifting sands. If the first truck got stuck, the others would immediately stop and back away. Then, of course, everyone would have to get out and help dig or push the truck out of the sand, sometimes with the assistance of metal plates, which were brought along for that exact purpose. During precarious situations, everyone had to carry their own stuff and walk in the dangerous temperatures.

If the ground was hard enough, they would speed along until the inevitable happened: the first truck getting stuck in a soft patch of sand. This happened early in the journey, and when it did, the second truck almost hit the first. The driver braked so hard that Robel, who was standing in the middle of the truck bed along with five other people, was thrown out. As a consequence, the first truck broke its crankshaft, and one man broke his arm. A woman threw up because she had drunk too much water and not eaten enough food.

At night, they lined up the trucks, aimed into the direction of their journey, because by morning, the winds would have swept away the tire tracks, leaving everyone dangerously confused. Each refugee had brought their own food, and each morning at dawn, they would spontaneously share.

Prepared, the smugglers had brought a spare crankshaft, but it took a full day to replace the damaged one. "If we don't have mechanics in our group, we not make it." While the smugglers had some skills, Robel described them as "not knowing so much."

The man with the broken arm used a cotton T-shirt to tie it up. After the crisis, they drove on amongst dust devils and scorching-hot ground temperatures.

DEHY
Location: Sahara
Interview: 9:33 a.m., September 11, 2012, Strawberry
Starbucks, Mill Valley, CA

Robel rode in the middle truck, crossing the Sahara. "It is [amazing] place. Once you in it, you feel like big big world is like Sahara. Ya."

There might be 100 miles of flat earth, then suddenly you are abruptly confronted with giant sand dunes. If the dunes blocked the travelers, they had no choice but to drive around them. Sometimes it would take a whole day only to discover that the new way was blocked too, and you'd just spent all that time (precious water, gas, and food) going in the wrong direction. Then they would have to double back. "Compass don't help if your way blocked."

"One crazy day, first truck getting in trouble as usual," Robel picked up the story at our weekly coffee shop meeting. "This time it stuck in sand all way up door." He measured his words for emphasis and leveled his hand in the air to illustrate. "We spent *whole day* trying get Toyota truck out of sand." The frustration was still evident in Robel's voice as he spoke, a million miles and days later. "… and ya, front tire only 25 percent full of air most of time but it stuck anyway. Then we have … ya, push it [backwards] out of dunes … find a new way. You not go forward, because it always be worse. Then you trapped and die."

On second week, second truck broke. Piston. They could see one piston not worked … they could see it! But we make it work without. The truck not going fast, and it damage other pistons, but we keep going.

"The scariest week, when we running out water *and* lost direction." Robel lowered and slowly shook his head, remembering.

On previous crossings, "[smugglers] left tires and sheet metal in sand," he motions upright.

> These are, ya … our gas stations. Sometimes clothes tied on metal. So every three or four days we have find our gas stations. Ya … these are our [markers] in big big desert. For two days we lost … not finding our gas station. We running out of gas. We lost? Or did other men [smugglers or robbers] find our station?

They were supposed to cross their region of the Sahara in two weeks, but they kept getting lost. By the third week, no one had any water left. Finding and counting on an oasis was vital to everyone's survival, but it was like finding a needle in a haystack. With only a compass and the sun (when it wasn't overcast) to guide them, it was easy to overshoot a small patch of date palms.

"… By time we completely out water," Robel told me in a raised voice, "we passed dehy and we looking death. Our lips cracked. Bleeding. We can't talk."

YODIT
Location: Sahara
Interview: 9:33 a.m., September 28, 2012, Strawberry
Starbucks, Mill Valley, CA

With his eyes closed, lips stuck together, and head bobbing to the rhythm of the truck, Robel sought inwardly to find some comfort. His mind returned to the first time he saw Yodit. It was at a dinner party, at the home of one of his uncle's trucking colleagues in Sudan. Yodit was helping her mother cook. She was pretty and he was taken with her soft and respectful voice. After dinner, while the adults were involved with their conversations and not paying attention, Robel and Yodit were able to chat a little and get to know each other. She was in high school.

"If you don't mind, can I get your phone number?," Robel asked. Because Yodit knew Robel's uncle and the families were close, she felt safe around him. There wasn't any pressure, so she secretly wrote it down on a bit of paper and slipped it to him. He couldn't wait and called that night. In his words they "make polite [small] talk."

Robel's uncle, Arefine, had a daughter named Abrehet, who was Yodit's classmate. While living with his uncle, Robel asked his cousin Abrehet to visit and invite Yodit to come along. It was the perfect excuse to see her again. When Abrehet proposed the visit to Yodit, the next day at school, she was excited about the idea. Abrehet quickly became the bridge (and chaperone) for a very shy Yodit to get to know Robel better. When Abrehet disclosed that Robel really liked her, the news embarrassed Yodit, but secretly, she also liked it.

Robel's strategy was simple: He took every opportunity to call and court her. Abrehet accompanied him when he visited Yodit at her high school. They drank tea or juice together, and

41

sometimes Abrehet left them alone for a few minutes of privacy. He called her several times per week. Sometimes Yodit "visit Abrehet" at her home with Robel there. The three of them drank tea, shared bread, watched television, told jokes, and just hung out. Afterwards they walked Yodit home and chatted the whole way. Despite being Christian, in public, the young women dressed piously with their hair and everything from neck down hidden under their *tarhah* (head and shoulder cover) and *abaya* (cloak).

Robel said he would have called or visited with her every night if he could have afforded it.

One day, Abrehet was sick and stayed home from school. Robel walked a long way to meet Yodit and, on the way home, stopped by a restaurant and had lunch with her. Robel told her he was in love with her and that it was his intention to marry her. Not right away, but in the future. —And forever.

She knew it was coming and said she had to think about it. "If I do," Yodit continued, "I have to tell my parents about it and see what they say."

The next few days, Robel tried to call her, but the phone was blocked. Ouch! Then it was out of service. For three days, he called every half hour or so. Damn. What happened? He was sure he was officially rejected. By her? By her parents?

Abrehet eventually put an end to his misery by calling him. "She say fine. Nothing new. Don't worry. I can relax, Yodit's phone broken, is all." That coming Friday was a holiday, and Yodit invited Robel (via Abrehet) to meet again at a cafeteria. They lingered there all day, and it was beautiful.

Yodit's answer was *yes* to his marriage proposal. However, there was a procedure they had to follow. It was a matter of tradition. First, he must go to her parents and ask both of them for her hand in marriage. She would also have to finish high school. Finally, Robel would have to secure a job.

Robel was elated and said he would fulfill her criteria, one at a time, as long as her answer remained yes. "To begin," Robel told me,

> I'm very shy and have talk my uncle. I so in love with her and want make her my wife. Want marry her. I more nervous wreck than even asking her. My uncle and her parents like top CEO. If they say no, it over.

His uncle came home from work at 4:30 p.m. and asked Robel if he was OK. Robel nervously replied, "This is how it is, your friend daughter … I love her. We agreed marry as long as you and her parents agree." To which his uncle replied, "I'm glad it's not something else. This is a problem we can solve."

The next day, both Robel's uncle and Yodit's father had a day off from work and met at Yodit's home for a conversation about the couple. Robel went to his new construction job.

The meeting went well with her parents, and they reiterated that she must finish school first. The couple had to wait. The adults agreed to the plan: to have an engagement party in about a month's time. Yodit and her mother picked out the gold engagement ring at a local jewelry store. The party's theme was pink and so was the dress. "Now. Here we go!," recalled Robel, "She my *fiancé* and I her *fiancé*."

He was 22 years old and she, 17.

They had the party. She continued to go to high school. Robel decided to leave Sudan.

> My promise is this -- as long as God survive me this trip, I be beneficial her. Find nice place live. Italy first, but not good place. My journey not over. USA political asylum. I complete in one year. Get green card, travel paper. January 17, 2010, in Sudan, we planning getting married. Over 2,000 people come.

43

DEATH
Location: Sahara
Interview: 10:00 a.m., September 11, 2012, Strawberry
Starbucks, Mill Valley, CA

"In three weeks, three days, and around 3:00, we find oasis.
Ya. I remember this. Exact."

Five palm trees were spotted in a slight depression, and the
drivers shouted with excitement. "We saved! Everyone so
happy. We thanks God. We saved."

I take a sip of my morning coffee and prepare to type quickly
on my portable keyboard to capture Robel's exact words as he
relived the transition from desperation to salvation,

> When you dry, water, you don't have water and you uh
> … [he mimics being unable to swallow] dehy
> everythings, dry the mouth, is already bloody and dry.
> Then we find oasis water, and everybody so excited
> jumping out of truck and five guys get … find, [uses his
> hands to pantomime a container], taking ["container?" I
> offer], ya, over here trees, [hand circles around] it. Look
> like natural -- cornered by sand. Kind of dry rock. Sand
> doesn't come there pretty much. Oh … look like
> someone digging hole. Water dropping into hole. Like
> kind of little water. Little stream. Kind of [we discuss the
> word "spring"]. Con-tai-ner … ya … one climbed inside
> and got big con-tai-ner and everyone drink and drink
> and drink.
>
> Driver run but it too late. Everyone drink and drink…
> Too much water! Hole maybe five, six feet deep. Thirty
> to 40 inches water. If you down water you have waiting.

It took about one minute to collect one ounce of water from the
seeping sides of the hole in the earth. The man in charge

warned everyone not to drink too much. But the first five men did anyway. He tried to control them by holding their containers and counting, "one thousand one, one thousand two, one thousand three, one thousand four, one thousand five. Then "Next!' " But some of the men wouldn't control themselves. They drank too much, too fast, and the inevitable happened: water intoxication, then death.

"Womans cry all night. We have two holy men who pray almost two hours." Robel said in a soft voice "Night, we eating our food, drink from hole, cry and pray."

In the morning, they scooped out a place in the sand and buried all five of them. I asked Robel if it was within sight of the oasis. "No, we carry them. Ya, maybe two miles carry."

Was there a grave marker? "Metal things we just put on side and put name by [writing in charcoal]. Metal very wide. Like board [sheet metal].

How many men worked on the grave? "Almost 35 people. It is what it is," Robel recalled, "You take risk in life. You don't know what is your fate."

"We don't have resting at Oasis *because it is a dangerous place,"* Robel remembered. *"*We have leave. Lots of robbers come here too. Everyone comes here."

They left by 10:30 a.m. with all the water that they could carry. Even though they were close to the Libyan border, they lost two more days. The guides couldn't locate the aluminum trash markers that had been previously laid out to show a guideline pointing out of the Sahara in the direction of Libya and Egypt. So close and yet so far away! They even backtracked towards the oasis for a full day, in an attempt to start over and get the correct bearing.

Approximately two days before they reached the city of Koufra, they tied up several barrels of fuel. Next, the men dug a deep hole to bury the barrels for the return trip. They used tire rims, clothes, and aluminum to mark the spot in the barren wasteland.

"What prevents others from seeing these markers and digging for the fuel?," I asked Robel. "Ahhh, you don't put mark on top of treasure, but maybe 50 feet away." They buried over 120 gallons of gas.

"On way back Libya," Robel continued, "there not be people on trucks. Just gas. They use buried gas stations all way back Sudan border." The gas stations could be buried in all types of terrain: hard-packed earth, sand dunes, rocks, and gravel pits.

The Sahara is subdivided into deserts with different countries and geographical characteristics. It took over three weeks to reach an oasis and one month to cross the treacherous desert.

LIBYA

KOUFRA, LIBYA
Location: Sahara

I found myself fascinated with how many ways there were to spell many of the locations within this story. Koufra for example, can be found with these various spellings: Kufra, Cufra, Khofra, Al Kufrah, and Koufra. How would I choose? I asked Robel how he spelled it. He didn't know.

Koufra, is a group of oasis' in the heart of the Saharan desert. The village of Kufra, because of its geographical location, has always been a popular, albeit traditional stop for refugees and migrants. Unfortunately vulnerable travelers also attract criminals and traffickers looking for oportunities to exploit them.

> When we reaching Koufra, we celebrate. It midnight and we … ya, they take us big house. Back yard. No one, *especially police,* seeing us. They put big carpet in yard and cover [cloth screen] over our heads. We sleep five hours, then we can travel at five in morning, before police or people of city see us.
>
> They mostly white. We don't look like them. Our language different too. The Libyan blacks we see, darker skin than us. We illegal. If we not hiding, someone ask see documents.

Before daybreak, the 75 Eritrean refugees comprised of women, children and men, were woken up. The original agreement was that the money they paid would take them all the way to Tripoli, the capital and largest city in Libya, located on the Mediterranean Sea. It was 4:00 a.m. and,

"Now we… [discover] if we want make it from Koufra to Tripoli, we have pay more. Three hundred dollars more!," Robel said angrily.

> Ya. We don't know this going happen. If people don't have it, they have borrow. They [transporters] know *one hundred percent* everyone have money but don't plan using it. They say us, if we argue them, we have pay extra. If you don't pay, we give you police.

Robel speculated that friends of the transporters who had joined the group were getting a free ride, with everyone else making up the difference.

> Here's the thing: It's a game. At six in morning it's light. Everyone can see you. After five miles from Koufra, they stopping all trucks. Five or six police cars [circling motions with his hands] our three trucks. They know we leaving. Police waiting. For us! They see open truck, bunch of people. Seventy-five people! Everyone pay extra money. We are busted. They also arrest drivers. Everyone went jail in Koufra. Except drivers. We don't see them there.

PRISON
Koufra, Libya
Interview: 10:10 a.m., October 8, 2012, Strawberry Starbucks,
Mill Valley, CA

I believe *arrest* of truck drivers fake. They put us in one
police car and truck drivers, together, in other police car,
ya. We all go back to Koufra and held in immigration.
Maybe police went to different exit and they do it again
with next people.

At that time, the government of Eritrea was best friends with
Libya, so it might take a while, but Robel suspected that it
would probably end in deportation. If Robel were deported to
Eritrea, he would most likely face death for being a deserter.

The holding pen consisted of a huge backyard utilizing the
blank faces of buildings plus a fence to enclose them. Each
person was interrogated one by one: "How did you get here?
How long did it take? How many people? How much money?
Who were the drivers? Why did you leave?" Robel said there
was nothing to do but tell the truth. He told them everything,
starting with running away from the army and ending up in jail.

The group lived outside. The corrugated aluminum roof kept
the hot sun off of them. All their personal possessions had
been confiscated. There were lots of little mats to sleep on.
They ate bread and steamed rice with a cup of tea and milk.
Dinner consisted of lentil soup with bread. On Fridays, they
had meat. The food was welcome but not particularly good.

After two days, they were declared illegal immigrants and
would have to stay in custody.

They don't say us what happens. They [he used the
palm of his hands to pantomime separating] boys from
girls. Children go with womans into other house

[building]. Three people in room. Six or seven rooms. Our beds made from three levels [stacked] cement blocks. Cement gets very cold at night. [He hugged himself.] We have small, thin [foam rubber] mat and one blanket. No pillow. The bed hard!

Three doors on building and all locked. Some rooms bigger and they have six people. We only three in our cell because it's small. There one [open-air] window with bars. We only see others at breakfast, lunch, dinner.

I asked Robel, specifically, if it was freezing at night. His eyes got big as he nodded his head and mumbled affirmatively with "Oh my God."

The courtyard included seats and picnic tables. They picked up food next to the kitchen. The refugees only had 10 to 20 minutes to eat. They weren't allowed to socialize.

We in this prison for six months! There no one, and no way, to contact anyone. We only talking and exercise in our room.

Teame, one of Robel's cell mates, took a turn for the worse.

He really sick. One day he not wakes up. The guard push him ... go breakfast ... but he don't move. He only little breathing. An ambulance come. He have stone. [Robel points to his kidney.] He needs cut open, get stone out. He gone for month. They good care him at hospital. He watch TV and learned what going on in world.

Berhe, the other cellmate, was very quiet; always praying.

He very close becoming priest. He prayed all day. I prayed with him a lot. It really peaceful. No choice. Worrying doesn't change anything. All we can do ...

50

pray and relax ourself. What has happened to our roommate when they taking him away? It big question for a month.

When Teame returned from the hospital, Robel felt *a little free*. Robel and Berhe felt like they had a visitor from the outside world. He was chatting all day and night about what was happening in the world. Teame looked good and healthy.

So he explain us a lot of things. Sooner or later, we get deport. We don't know what about world and what is happen.

What's point of keeping us for months and struggle all our lifes? Why not deport us now? Maybe one week after Teame return us, there big, big immigration meeting. They talking all prisoners. They talking plan, what it look like. What they will do for us ... or not.

They say us, they keeping everyone there for more invest-ti-ga-tion. To see how they be sent back safe. Or, there another option. If each person paid $700, they just open door and let [you] out to *see what you can do*. Whoever want pay this money ... uh ... invited to come to office.

A lot of people didn't have the money. Robel had $1,200 sewn into his pants waistline. "So I'm first person in office. I show them in office I have $800 and say them 'All I have,' so they don't think I have more and they ask for more and more."

Robel knew what would happen to him if he were deported. This was the only way. The prison gave him the option to go to Tripoli and get a "green pass." He would be able to go by bus and be armed with a letter of permission, in case he was stopped on the road by the police. There were a lot of checkpoints between Koufra and Tripoli. So Robel set his sights on Tripoli and Port Tunisia. Out of 75 people who had crossed the great Sahara Desert together, only one other man, named Eyob, and one woman, left with Robel.

FROM KOUFRA PRISON TO TRIPOLI AND ZUWARA,
LIBYA
Interview: 10:20 a.m., December 10, 2012, Strawberry
Starbucks, Mill Valley, CA

Robel plus two other people paid for and were given a "green
paper" to travel by bus to Tripoli. Who knew where the money
for the green papers went [Robel speculated]: into the pockets
of the prison officials? A little to the government? Of course,
there was no receipt to investigate.

They were safe, and they were legal in terms of traveling. At
least for the moment. The bus trip took all day. They made
stops in Benghazi (the second largest city in Libya) at
restaurants and service stations, and stayed no more than a
half hour. They left the prison around six that morning and
arrived in Tripoli, the capital and largest city of Libya, around
seven in the evening.

Robel paid an Egyptian restaurant to allow him to use a phone
and contact a friend in Tripoli. Mebrahtu had traveled before
him (also from Sudan), using the same route but without the
difficulties.

Mebrahtu picked up Robel and took him to his rental home.
The plan was that Robel and Eyob would rent rooms in the
city and be Mebrahtu's housemates.
Once settled, Robel called Uncle Arefine and asked him to
wire money to Tripoli. He needed money because the green
papers that he'd been given in prison would expire in two
weeks and were only good for traveling, not employment or
being able to take up residency.

During this time, Tripoli (including its surrounding metropolitan
areas) had a population, of well over a million. Robel
described it as a place where one could maneuver. "No one
ask papers unless you wrong place, wrong time."

Arefine sent $1,800.

The plan: "We looking for someone provide us Mediterranean passage." Robel continued,

> There is an Eritrean person, a broker, who works with Libyan citizen, who does [preparing] the boat, how you cross by the sea. They put three 'flatables on top fishing boat. They drop you close Sicily, at deserted beach so no one sees you. Each 'flatable holds … maybe … 20 people. The big boats cannot get close to land.

They found that broker.

> We pay $1,200 [each] to one person who buy us place on boat. We are 120 people. No stuff [provisions]. Have buy your *own* life jacket. Bring your *own* [survival gear]. We taken 20 [at a time] by mini [bus] to Zuwara … small town west of Tripoli, on border Tunisia. At dock they tell, waiting us in con-tai-ner, ya …120-130 of us went into this place. One door. It locked behind. We more afraid of police than getting in box. We scary loosing all money. We don't even talk.

The guards at the dock were paid to look the other way.

FIRST MEDITERRANEAN CROSSING
Location: From Tripoli, Libya to Crossing the Mediterranean
Interview: 9:52 a.m., December 17, 2012, Strawberry
Starbucks, Mill Valley, CA

They waited at a farm house by the sea. The wooden storage
shed that everyone was squeezed into was one big, empty
shed, amongst many. Roughly 50 people came from Eritrea
and the rest from Egypt. I asked Robel to compare the size of
the shed to the Starbucks that we were sitting in, here in
California, and he said it was about the same.

The hours grew. They had entered the shed waiting for the
correct shift of night guardsmen to be on duty: the ones who
were trusted enough to be bribed. The timing was crucial. The
wait expanded throughout the night and into the next day.
There wasn't a bathroom, and yet no one relieved themselves
on the cement floor.

The man they paid eventually showed up with a truck and
three brothers. They brought food for everyone: soda, cheese,
crackers, bread, and water. Robel reflected on the fact that,
considering the amount of money everyone had paid, the food
didn't even look like it had amounted to $100 worth.

"Why you keeping us here?," they asked. It was not part of the
plan to be locked up. Unfortunately, they were told, they would
have to wait.

It took almost 26 hours before they received the first update:
The fishing boat from Tunisia was coming. Everyone hurried
up and prepared, then waited some more. Around midnight,
the ship was in the vicinity, and they were ready to mobilize.

The organizer and his brothers escorted them, 20 at-a-time,
on the 20-minute walk to the sea. Robel was in the second
group. Everyone was carefully quiet. They walked in single file

to avoid the huge lights that were placed everywhere in the farm center to deter just this type of clandestine activity. There was only a small window of opportunity, because of the changing of the guards as well as the course that the ship would have to take, to avoid detection and inspection.

The fishing boat had to leave by 2:00 a.m. or they would get caught. The problem was that Libya has a huge offshore oil refinery platform about 60 miles out. The boat would be able to see the lights and give it a wide berth. Otherwise, once day broke, the refinery would spot the vessel and investigate. So the men in charge of their passage to the fishing boat were snapping their fingers, insisting, "Let's go, let's go!," to speed things up. When they reached the shore, two of the brothers separated out 10 people each into two small inflatable boats. *There were lots of women and children,* Robel recalls.

Small motors, attached to their inflatables, expedited their crossing to the huge fishing boat that was quietly waiting for them in the dark.

It took Robel about 10-15 minutes to arrive at the ship. The vessel had three levels. The lowest level normally held fish, but for this trip it was empty except for the stench that wafted up. The middle level held bunk beds. On the top floor was the kitchen, occupied mostly by the Tunisian captain and his crew of seven. At the back deck of the ship were three inflatables ready to transport roughly 25 people each. The rest of the deck was empty.

The Eritreans and Egyptians made themselves comfortable in three levels of bunk beds. Robel took a middle bunk. It had a pillow, sheets, and a blanket. At two in the morning, they launched and, soon after, successfully circumvented the refinery in the distance.

During the passage, they ate their own food. Between the stench and seasickness, Robel was lucky to vomit only once, but others were sick the whole time. Some of the passengers chatted with the crew members. Some wandered around. Everyone tried to relax.

By the third day, they had traveled through (what Robel referred to as) the Libyan sea into the Mediterranean's international waters. When they reached the border of Italian waters, the captain turned off the motor and scoped out the situation. Everyone stood around smoking and assessing. They needed to wait for nightfall to take the passengers to shore in secret.

Out of nowhere, the Italian coast guard arrived en masse; helicopters and boats were suddenly everywhere. They thought the boat needed rescuing since it was just sitting there, dead in the water. A bullhorn erupted with a command to STOP, just as the captain got scared and turned on the motor to flee.

Chaos broke out all over the ship. The captain and his crew wanted to get out of there before they were caught hauling human cargo. At a minimum, they would lose their fishing license and never be able to return to Italy for shipping business. The Egyptian passengers were on the side of the captain. If they were caught, they would be deported back to Egypt, facing their punishment for illegally leaving their country. The Eritreans, on the other hand, were legitimate refugees and *wanted* to get caught by the Italians because they would be given asylum by the government. It was a recipe for disaster.

Robel and six other Eritreans tried to open the captain's door to persuade him to let them go. The act was seen as hostile by the crew, and tear gas was used directly on them. It took Robel three hours to be able to open his eyes again.

Meanwhile, the Italians stopped pursuing the fishing boat as it crossed back into international waters. The captain told everyone to calm down and explained: He had a wife and seven kids to worry about. He couldn't lose his fishing livelihood. He had made a promise to drop them off in a safe place and would honor that.

At around 9:00 p.m., everyone was exhausted and tried to sleep.

> Captain have big knife. Pepper spray. He don't wanna stop. Guard keep follow him, kick out of Italian sea. Almost two, three hours. Try kicked out of water. Cannot follow. We spend all night and day in international water. That's the day, uh ... in a day, the captain promise us, he *will* do his job. Right thinking. Getting us safe without caught his ship. Then we talk him. He gonna do that.
>
> He chillin.' Good day in international water. He give us beer. Day that we gonna be relaxed. The day become dark and try to start going. We don't know which direction anyway. He gonna take us some island Italy. After all night traveling. Sometime around three or four in morning. Plastic boats, using all seven people that work with him to take them down.

Around three in the morning, the announcement was made: Lights had been spotted on the Italian coast, and they were told to get ready. The inflatables took about one-half hour to transport 25 people at a time to the shore. The total operation took almost two hours. The captain said "Good luck, bye-bye," and disappeared into the night.

Some people took off running the second they hit the ground, but Robel and his compatriots remained. As darkness lifted, they could make out that they were on an open beach with plastic water bottles, cigarettes, various pieces of garbage and flotsam strewn everywhere.

So this was what Italy looks like, Robel thought. The freedom and relief that everyone felt was like "we are in heaven. The angels looked us." Many dropped to their knees and prayed.

"First, we thanks God," Robel recalled. Several people cried tears of joy.

They decided they would pick a direction and walk until they met someone. There was a huge building (oil refinery?) in the distance, on the beach. Someone questioned the green flag planted in front of a guardhouse. Was *that* the green flag of Italy?

"Ya, ya," one of the Eritreans offered. "My sister, who lives there, told me, this is the Italian green." They continued walking towards the building. A man dressed in sandals and civilian clothes, who looked to be in his 50s, stepped out of the security hut and walked towards them. When they met, the Eritreans heard his morning greeting, "As-salamu alaykum," and were stunned.

Some in the group collapsed. Others froze with their mouth wide open. Women started crying. Robel cast his eyes down into his coffee as he remembered, "It very, very sad. I only one speaking Arabic … but everyone understand."

The man asked what was going on, and Robel explained: They had come from Eritrea, having crossed the great Sahara Desert and spent over three days crossing the sea. They had each paid $1,200. They were supposed to be dropped off in Italy.

"Oh my god," the soldier replied in sympathy. "I'm so sorry what happened. This not Italy. This Tunisia. You border Zuwara. Libya is, ya … 10 miles from here. You make circle."

The security guard could have used his gun to arrest them all, but he was a kind man. Instead, he told them to run away immediately.

> You have disappear. This never happened here before. You have say your organizer, your broker. But you

must run before anyone see you. You will go prison and if deport, maayyybeeee even death.

The womans cried. All of men very, very angry.

They looked around at the fine sand and semi-desert terrain. Because of the passing cars, they could see the freeway that led straight from Tunisia to Libya. "Some people run away, wherever," Robel explained. The remaining thirty-or-so people hid under the trees neighboring the highway, to regroup and think.

It was October of 2003.

THE PROVIDER AND THE COFFEE SHOP
Location: Libya/Tunisian Border to Crossing the
Mediterranean
Interview: 9:45 a.m., December 24, 2013, Strawberry
Starbucks, Mill Valley, CA

The next time I met Robel at the Strawberry coffee shop, it
was buzzing with students and parents who were off for the
December holidays. Robel reiterated where he'd left off in his
story. "Looking at oil refinery, there … see flag and guard in
[front of] building. One Eritrean, he just make believe himself it
Italian flag. 'No, no, I have sister in Italy, she say Italian green
flag.' Then security guard say us good morning, what's going
on, in Arabic." Robel shook his head as he remembered the
utterly devastating folly.

After they hid in the trees by the motorway, Robel used a cell
phone and his Arabic language skills to call the "person who
provide us all the trip." Robel continued:

> We maybe 10 to 20 miles from Zuwara - from place we
> start. A very bad situation. The broker say us 'do not
> move!' He coming with two minibuses. When he
> arriving us, we jump out of trees. Then he speeding to
> his house in Zuwara. It have big walls. We hiding there
> three days. Sleeping on floor. We eat a lot of bread.
> Two people [at a time] leave getting food. After two
> days, we hear news: A West African boat also going
> Italy, carry 200 people, and they all die in the sea.
> Same sea! *Too many people and too many waves.*

While they waited at the safe house, the Eritrean government
officially asked Libya to help stop all attempts at such
Mediterranean passages. In Zuwara, the police began a
sweep: They were going to every single house to look for
refugees. Robel explained that the European Union was
putting international pressure on Libya in terms of human

rights. Zuwara in particular was famous for being a source of illegal immigration. Representatives of the European Union human rights were coming to Zuwara to look firsthand at the situation. So the sweep was an attempt to clean things up before they got there.

Like a fish in the sea, Robel got caught in the net. He knew that if he resisted, he would get arrested, so "I not resist."

On the bus, Robel recalls:

> We thinking they deporting us. Worse thinking was prison or die in Eritrea. It most sadness ever. Ever. We crossing Sahara and crossing Mediterranean. We go so far.
>
> They driving past city of Tripoli. We see immigrant town with shopping, restaurants. I think … we close to Tripoli. A shopping [district]? All different types of immigrants. They let us out. They just wanted rid us in Zuwara. But they don't want anything to do with us. To help us.

Robel got in touch with Mebrahtu in Tripoli. His friend was shocked at what had happened. Robel stayed with him, but at this point, he only had money left for food, but not another attempt at crossing the Mediterranean.

SECOND MEDETERRANEAN CROSSING

So second time we in Tripoli and we keep back café, asking broker, he need sending us again. He say us, "I don't have any idea and have to ask. Zwara. Ask boss. After two days I come back, and I give you answer."

His boss say, 'Nothing he can do at moment, but if … *if* they really want go, *I* can get a boat, and *I* send them.'

And we, as group, agree go because every time it can be worse. It better take chance. Leave Tripoli. OK then … we set up again. We are 30 Eritrean people. Five people from Bangladesh.

So and … uh, one of the Bangladesh guy call provider and say him, "I was a captain." And with his four friends, they can go by us for free, because if you captain, you allowed have some people go with you without pay. They might pay to him, Bangladeshi guy.

Robel shrugs.

And so we going that day. Ya … at night we start travel by minibus. Around four thirty afternoon, direction Zuwara. So between Zuwara and Tripoli. Masarada? Not sure that name. Then they place for you. You know, little house for gardener. Farmer. They keeping us there almost dark, and the boat ready. A little small boat that to carry to big boat, for five people. To big plastic boat for 35 people. So they keeping transfer us. Five minutes from farm to sea. Small plastic boat to big plastic boat.

Journey is started, little past midnight. For 30 people, but we was 35! Ya … and you know, Bangladesh captain is not really experience, don't know how to ride

63

[drive] it. Too slow. Too heavy for boat. And power engine is not strong that driving boat. Almost 80 or 90 miles, ya, out of sea and we side [parallel] Libyan refinery. As soon we there, BAM! the air is blown up on one side. Then it nine in the morning. Nothing we can do. And we have cell phone. International phone with us. I only... I only speak Arabic. I call Libyan provider. Something wrong. Call me. We say him, side of the boat broke. No air. Leak.

He say us "don't guys move." He say [ask] me where? As soon as we have ... we have ... not smart GPS like today.

"Compass?, " I offered Robel as he struggles in his excitement of retelling the story, while trying to find the words in English.

Yes! Compass. Read direction. And I have go. Sit, where captain at. Say him, 90 degrees north. East. I might. Don't read exactly? Waiting five or six hours and nobody coming. Northeast?

No ... body.

So after that, we decide. Go back. Around, one-thirty, one afternoon. And then we have, uh, life jacket now. Body. Most of womans crying, and we think it's just not going to get aways from this and so, most boys have life jacket, go deep in sea.

Robel motions with his palms up under his chin.

Keep driving with motor on. Other guys on side. Ladies on side. We are in sea on broken side and we have to [mimics lifting] flat plastic out of water.

We keep going back Zuwara. After 12 hours in water, we don't move pretty much. We back right next refinery on land. Where dumped first time and thinking Italy.

Then police come us with pickup car. As soon we get there, we leave the thing and run away. Fourteen people arrest. They got them. Me and friends, we run away, and we stay on a, on a ... under the forest. For almost all day. Then after getting dark, we went to Zuwara 'cause we can see lights. We rent a taxi. Go back to Tripoli. Then when I stay there, with my friend.

Two days later, we going broker and we ask him if he can do something else. He say me, let me ask the boss. We say OK, and after two days we meet and go back and see. No ... have waiting. When arrest, someone tell who provider. So provider is dealing with people in jail.

But it takes time, and you gotta pay money. Jail. Ya. Meet right people. Let them out. It taking him two weeks. He take them out of jail. He very nice guy. According to, compare to, other providers, he nice.

After everybody comes out of jail, we go broker, what we gonna do. Boss say us, he can credit.

The broker spoke with the provider, but was not able to refund the money. However, he had permission to credit everyone $700. But there were strings: *each* refugee would have to add an additional $600 cash and recruit 10 new people. The new people would pay the full amount in cash, which was $1,300. That was the minimum for Robel to attempt yet another passage across the sea to Italy.

THIRD MEDITERRANEAN CROSSING: THE LITTLE
WOODEN BOAT
Locations: Tripoli, Zuwara, Libya
Lampedusa & Croten, Italy
Interview: 10:00 a.m., January 7, 2013, Strawberry Starbucks,
Mill Valley, CA

"How did you find that many more people??," I asked,
incredulous. "Ya," Robel chuckled, "that's good question."

They put the word out in the Eritrean community and
advertised by word of mouth. In Robel's refugee circle, there
were already 50 people. It quickly grew by 20 more, which is,
as Robel described it, "Very positive sounding." In other words,
despite what happened during the previous attempts
(including the unrelated boat that sank and killed 200
migrants), the sheer amount of refugees that were interested
in trying it again sounded encouraging and inspired
confidence in the newcomers.

I asked for more details on how it all worked, especially since
cash was involved. Robel said that after someone expressed
an interest, they were taken to the broker or provider. There,
they purchased a ticket, which was simply a hand- written
receipt. Their name was entered into a passenger ledger.

> Many people in the Eritrean community. They help us.
> People don't want stay there [Libya]. It's not safe.
> Maybe police come, they arrest you. The provider is
> good person. He has good reputation. Now is chance.
> Someone else can take the money and run.

The whole recruitment process took about two weeks.

The broker announced that they had reached the goal of 70
new people, and it was time to go. It took four to five days to

arrange. "Which way better? Who, what, from where, and what time?"

The third plan for the clandestine immigration was basically the same. A minibus took them west, along the coastal route from Tripoli to Zuwara, to the same house. This time, however, the provider had to guess at boat capacity. The specifications were not always accurate. Tunisia was the place to purchase cheap and cheaply built boats, which is what he did. It was small, open and this time, made of wood. And it was supposed to hold the 120 people.

At this point, I interrupted Robel's story to tell him about a 3-D movie I'd just seen called, "Life of Pi" by Ang Lee, which came out in 2012 and was based on Yann Martel's novel of the same name. I wanted to know if his boat looked at all like the open, wooden boat in the movie. I also wondered if anything else from the fantasy film resonated with him and his story, especially the vulnerability of being out in the open air and sea. He hadn't seen the movie, but promised he would.

At our next coffee shop meeting, Robel enthusiastically confirmed there were many similarities, especially the boat in the movie, which looked exactly like his, except smaller. He also said his wife had to cover her eyes several times in the theater, because the special effects were so realistic, they frightened her.

I asked Robel again how many people were squeezed into that small boat? About 135. So how high off the water was the edge of the boat? He estimated only about two to three feet above the sea level.

"That's why so many people [end up] in Malta," he told me,

> ... because when wave is coming it's *hard* crossing Italy. Malta is in middle of. If wave coming, it's easy go there and save your life. If wave, sooner or later you gonna die. If you smart, you turn there. It's right there. Not *that*

far. Malta is an island. I don't know who own. Is it a country?

The assembly and holding areas for the immigrants were the same as before. The Libyan provider and his two brothers found a captain from Tunisia to be in charge, in exchange for gaining free passage to Italy. This time, unlike the fishing captain who did *not* want to be caught, the captain had the same goals as the Eritrean refugees: To be picked up by the Italian coast guard.

Robel gazed out of our coffee shop, across the highway and through the hill, often frequented by deer, and into an imaginary horizon line.

> You never … think to what happen in middle of sea. You always "what do I do NOW if the police comes?" Most people get caught before you get to sea. They pocket your money and put you in prison.

An inflatable plastic raft ferried them to the big, cheaply built wooden boat located about two miles from shore. It took three hours to get everyone shuttled out. The human traffickers didn't provide life preservers. If you wanted one, you had to purchase and bring your own. Robel didn't buy one because he had run out of money. It also seemed like a luxury and an afterthought compared to the logistics of having gotten thus far.

Robel gestured in the air, "Good luck. Bye-bye. Again at night. We have Yamaha engine. Starting like lawnmower." He pulled the imaginary cord. "Have to hide from the oil [platform rig] in the sea again. See it [motions hands in a circle]. This time it taking us 24 hours to reach the Italian sea."

Again, the Italian coast guard arrived in force. There was a "nice" huge boat. Helicopters too. The captain turned off the motor. Two ships braced their little wooden craft in between. Hands were extended, and everyone was pulled out one at a time.

"They save our lives. The Italians: our best guarantee. They always come to rescue us. I give them that credit." Robel looks away wistfully out of the picture window in our noisy coffee shop.

EUROPE

ITALY

The refugees were transported to a detention center on the little island of Lampedusa, which is a part of Sicily. Its official capacity at the time was for a maximum of 300 people. It was overcrowded.

They were herded into a large building that normally served as a food storage warehouse with offices. Women and children were separated from the men, so their clothes could be removed and everyone strip-searched for illegal drugs. The dirty clothes were incinerated and replaced with fresh throwaway paper clothes to be worn on the first day. "We wet, salty, and smell *bad*, and they don't have us showers," Robel shook his head, making a face.

They were given cheesecake, bread, and snacks. The communal area included chairs, but no windows or television. On the second day, their paper garments were swapped with regular street clothes. The refugees were locked in the warehouse for 2- ½ days.

The Italians brought in a helicopter to fly them to a refugee camp called, "Crotone".

I asked Robel if that was his first time in a helicopter. He laughed. "One colleague say "wow this is … oh we don't have a poorness anymore. From donkey to jumping in airplane." He from farm countryside. He don't even know car."

During the registration process, their names were entered into a computer. Women and children were again separated. Two people were assigned to "self driving camper," as Robel described them. Each camper had a small bathroom, a sink with water, and bunk beds. Families received bigger accommodations. The refugee camp was a very large facility, with hundreds of refugees.

I asked Robel what it was like living there. "Eating. Resting. Chillin."

The food trucks arrived, and everyone lined up for breakfast, lunch, and dinner. There were public showers and bathrooms. If you needed a blanket, you had to request it. Every week, you exchanged your linen.

After two months, everyone was finished with their interviews, fingerprinting, and processing of their case. The Italian government gave each refugee €1,500 in cash and a blanket for sleeping in the street. They were now free to be homeless.

"They let you out of camp, six or seven people [at a time]. Bye-bye, that's it."

The permits (*Permesso di Soggiorno*) represented a conundrum. "Official, you *cannot* work." Robel laid out the situation so that I could understand the dilemma that his freedom entailed. "So you find work illegal or leave Italy. But…"

A lot of the migrants had relatives to contact (and live with) in other countries: Germany, Sweden, England, UK, Norway, Denmark, and Poland.

> When you ask asylum, they fingerprint you. The fingerprint in computer, all Europe shares. They show your first country where you show up in, they deport you back that country, you arriving in. European community share fingerprint. Ya, they have agreement. Problem, Italy doesn't really want you.

"So how do they expect you to survive, if you are not allowed to work in Italy and all the other European countries deport you back to *your* point of entry, Italy?," I asked, confused.

Robel explained:

If people go to family, they can stay as *visitor* for one year. Ya, one year! Maybe you live with friends or family and help for free and they give place to live. Ya, feed you. But you must leave their country after one year [and stay away for a year], back to Italy and ask new permit ... ya, for year permit with Italian government. Italian permit, you to go anywhere except the United Kingdom. Permit does not allow working. So you have no money, no home. No future.

ROME
Location: Rome, Italy and surrounding areas
Interview: 9:30 a.m., January 14, 2013, Strawberry Starbucks,
Mill Valley, CA

Eventually, Robel finished the processing phase of the Italian
migrant camp, and it was time to go. They released seven
people at a time. Again, Robel dismissively waves in the air in
our coffee shop, "Good luck. Bye-bye." This time I understood
the absurdity of the wave.

"It 9:30 at night ..." Robel began again with a sip of coffee and
deep breath,

> You don't know where you are. It's soooo cold. They
> driving us town of Crotone ... one, two miles from camp.
> They drop us. We walk train station. I planned go Rome.
> I heard there places stay, but no organ-ni-zations
> helping you. The train that place at eleven night and we
> just missed. It very, very cold. There is no ... [he
> motions with his hands above his head to describe an
> awning], but it open air train station. In my backpack, I
> have biscotti, shoes, socks, underwear, clothes, Coke,
> toothbrush, and blanket they give us. We find ... ya ...
> *scatola di cartone* [cardboard boxes?, I ask] ya ...
> boxes in trash, put them on floor. Hard floor. Cement.
>
> After we out, we start spending night on train station
> building. And when we lying down on floor, on top
> *cartone*, one of our partners been asleep. Me and other
> friend who was, just you know, blanket on top, but we
> was just chillin.'
>
> Then after 30 minutes maybe 45 minutes later, a man
> come with black tie, wearing ... [Robel uses his hands
> on his leg to try and describe some type of clingy pants.
> Leggings? I pause to sip my coffee, thinking this can't

75

be right. So I describe what tights are. Really? Tights?]
ya … tights. And he have some jacket. I don't
remember what. Because it so cold. He was passed by.
Back and forth and back and forth us. Because you
know, we are colored. And he ask us where we came
from. He trying talking us. Trying … *you know*. But the
way he act was so weird us. He walk like woman. He
say us, "I'm gay." And we was so shocked because
pretty much … we don't even know the word.

Say us at camp. They say us the history [and culture of]
Europe at the camp. If they ask, don't be mad. Just be
politely and go on. It's first time in our life. There you go.
Most people come from Africa. You never see them in
your life. They give you, talking … how it is outside.

We just listen first one, and after that, we kind of ignore
him. Not interested. Talk. We are so tired. Trying rest.
Man we just passed through a lot of problems: sea,
deserts, but now end of the world see this kind of…

Robel trails off lost in his memory, searching for more
descriptive words, then finishes with, "Freezing cold. Don't
sleep good. We [shared] *cartone* like sardines in can."

The stiff and cold Eritreans woke up at five in the morning.
The next train was due to arrive at seven. Once the café
opened, they went inside and drank coffee, ate their breakfast,
and enjoyed the warmth. They bought their open seating
tickets for Rome from a machine.

We, ya … with cell phone, have friends from refugee
camp meet us Rome. From there, we go Eritrean
restaurant. Eat, hang out for three or four hours and
ask owner if we can shower. He say yes. We walk
around Roma Termini [railway station]. It have indoor
mall, over 100 shops! I sleep in west side [wing], in
corner, on the floor that night. It was store [doorway].

The [mall] heated and I sleep good until six in morning, when people starting their business day.

Friends come before us. Ya, they find us Catholic Church that provide us winter house. You must register. A translator say us it was 30-minute driving outside Rome. Like youth hostel. You get kicked out early in morning. Walk around village with nothing. Walking all day. Nothing to do. Waiting till open again at night. So we say him no. Now nine of us, all friends from the escape. All new friends.

Eventually Robel found a suitable place on the outskirts of Rome. The good news was that the location had transportation: the metro, trains, and buses. Out of financial necessity, they often took the trains without buying a ticket.

"Sometime, especially at end month, when they know people have no money, the ticket controller will try to *nail you* on the train," Robel laughs.

They had no money so, "What's to do?"

It was a €100 fine, but since no one had an address, there wasn't anywhere to send the ticket. The bad news is that Robel estimated that he received about two tickets per month.

During this period of living in the Catholic winter shelter, Robel didn't wander through his days aimlessly once he was kicked out at six in the morning. Instead he went to Italian language school.

ITALIAN LANGUAGE SCHOOL

It was around 2003 when Robel lived in the shelter from December through March, to get off the streets and out of the cold. During this time, Robel enjoyed the middle of a three-tier bunk bed and two square meals. Breakfasts consisted of pastries, coffee, tea, and milk.

"When you leave for day, you bring gloves, hat, jacket, everythings you need because you can't get back in." Six in the evening is when the doors opened for dinner. Food was served at 6:30 p.m. Dinner often consisted of pasta, spaghetti, lasagna, cooked vegetables, meat, fruit, soda, water, bread, tea, or coffee. Robel described it as "not too fancy." Some of the men staying there were Russian, Romanian, other Africans, Bangladeshis. Women, children, and families stayed at a different shelter. Robel recalled that winter as "crazy cold. Negative 2- or 6-degrees Celsius. It was only good situation because I staying out of cold."

With only 400 euro left, Robel was trying to save as much money as possible. "When I'm outside, I needed money for shoes, or call parents, but about food, we don't worry that much."

The refugees and immigrants hunted for food at other churches, and through networking, helped each other to remember what the limited hours were.

> One place in Piazza Venezia, you have to get there really early. Three lines. Sometimes they run out … shut door. Especially weekend. Even workers eat there, save money.

One of Robel's consistent friends was Tesfahiwet. They met on the same truck crossing the Sahara. But they didn't cross the Mediterranean together. Robel would have beaten him to

Italy if it hadn't been for being dumped back on the Tunisian/Libyan border during the first attempt. Tesfahiwet traveled with a different group, arrived at a different refugee camp, and lived in a different church shelter. Tesfahiwet and Robel found each other again at Rome's Termini Station. Robel remembered, "There is nothing to do at the heated terminal all day. Everyone finds everyone. Outside it is freaking cold." They became close friends and hung out together.

After the three coldest months in that region of Italy were over, everyone got "kicked out" of the house. The event was made less disappointing by way of a party with great food. The padre talked to over 60 people and gave advice on how to live beyond the shelter. "It's done. Winter is over."

Robel heard about more free Italian language classes. He also discovered there were other workshops available: *"lavoro di idraulico"* (plumbing), *"preparazione della pizza"* (pizza-making), *"mobili legno"* (furniture woodworking), and learning computer skills. His face lights up, and he chuckles as he uses a perfect Italian singsong intonation to name the disciplines.

One drawback to the free classes is that there was an age limit: 18 to 25 years old. Robel was 24. For three months, you could find him there, four days a week, studying two hours of Italian, two hours of plumbing, a lunch break, then two more hours of cooking. The lunches, he recalled enthusiastically, were:

> Free and fantastic. Oh, still I remember, a special chef. The cookin' was oah ... so good. Ya, we eat sometime twice times. Exciting to eat the food. Reaally, really good. They want to know all about our country. The Italian family owns Ferrari, Maserati and Fiat; they owned the building. Program. It was good time. I learned speak Italian just like that...

He snaps his fingers.

Robel took classes by day and lived on the streets by night. He was able to take showers at the school, where they provided soap and towels. I was surprised about the showers, so he explained:

> When you learn how making salami, you're all messed up from the head to toe! So they provide you lockers and showers.

> I also collect 50¢ from friends. I taking bus to laundromat and do all friends' laundry. My laundry too. Maybe one times a month. This helped. I still have a little money left from refugee camp.

> We walk *termini*, or take bus. The Roma Termini is open 24 hour, like giant mall, and warm. It never gets quiet until 11:30 at night.

To my delight, Robel breaks into a big grin and begins imitating the terminal's loudspeaker voice, giving instructions as to what train is on what track. His Italian accent is impeccable, and, judging by his chuckling, I can tell that he (and his friends) must have sat around doing this for their own amusement on many occasions.

> Then I hiding by door … uh office door. Ya, I have my [refugee] blanket. As long as you don't do something stupid, security don't bother you. The guards who walk don't care.

TIBURTINA: SQUAT NUMBER ONE

Robel and some friends found a *position of the government* that wanted to help them. They had a meeting with the Sinistra (leftist political party), which had an office next to the terminal. The Sinistra knew which government buildings around Rome were abandoned. They talked about a huge government storage building in the Tiburtina district. They also claimed that the Destra government [*Destra Liberale Italiano?*] was mafia influenced, "so they don't care about, or take care of the people."

I asked Robel if he thought the Sinistra was recruiting refugees for their own political promotion. He said, "Yes, of course. They trying brainwashing us. What is important is we promised housing, jobs, uh, refugees, by United Nations. Money was paid them [Italy] … but we are living in street with *nothing*."

He continued, "We supposed get working permits. As second options, we are Eritrean, which is basically…" He took a deep breath, paused and started over.

Italy is our second country because Italy agreed. Any country colonize Africa *must* give them citizenship! So we being treated same as immigrants [rather than] partner country and refugees. The Sinistra recruit you and you are probably a little bit mad at the Italian government. So what choice do you have?

We want same government as political party that talking us, and we want live in Tiburtina. We get bus. And they give us address and bus direct there. One of them, wear yellow thing, reflect. They can see everyone, airport. Bus. They stand looking. They waiting at destination. Some of them went to bus. At first we not a lot people when in this…

81

I describe the word "squat" to him as we sip our coffees on a chilly morning.

>Some went to gallery. Very big building. Only three level. In middle, nothing. Two sides. Three [he chops the air to symbolize three floors up]. Used to be place keeping for train stations. And water. Covered. But big hole. Has like, maybe eight, seven feet door. Eight feet. And so you have two, one [entry]. Then on side, [he chops the air again]. Middle nothing. See ... all the way [he points up].

>So anyway. Not a lot of people. Eritrean. Ethiopian. Moroccan. Ya, and some of them Romani. Some Russia. Sudanese. We be like over, like 70 people. But most Eritrean. We live about one year. Pretty much.

>When we occupy, police come. But we ready. We was waiting at door, and police there, 12 at night. But they don't want come us. Media there. Decide let us go. Keep watching out. They come at night maybe when we sleep. We have big chain ... can lock up door. We start living there. Steal electricity from wire outside. Putting electric entire hallway. [He chuckles.] Two shower. Everyone has waiting but ... So cold. Shower so cold. You don't have choice. People line, waiting, but so, so cold.

>Get garbage [he pantomimes a box]. Garbage box. Shred [tear] it. Separate it. Make a door to your private. [Separate] with cartone. No bed. Cartone. Blanket. Or you go to church. They give you blankets. And we don't have food. Go church, eating. But it's free. We don't have pay. We don't have money. [He shakes his head by swinging it like an infinity symbol.]

A woman, after that, she made a bar there. Grab all beer from supermarket and sell it there. Sandwich. Music. Income. Café.

Then I make a café. Hers is more bar. Mine: coffee and tea. Then me, after two week later, I start open my café and have restaurant/café. Not complete café or restaurant. Some breakfast. Selling a little cigarettes. Then I start beers ... You know they can eat ... drink a little wine. That's how I grow it up. Don't have much money at time. Growing a little. Making a little money. Buying all stuff. Selling, making money, buy more stuff.

In six month, I become good financial. So this, new people added, coming over and over. So the place getting busy. I start hire one lady. One man. And just pay them cash. And about, I was about one year. More people coming from sea. And place not enough. Squat not big enough.

THE COFFEE RITUAL

In back home, it is always the womans who does the coffee. One hundred percent … the woman. Not even young woman know how. The mom have teach them how serve the coffee.

First you have get fresh green bean of coffee. Make it ready. And with a charcoal of fire. On the con-tai-ner that hold the top … pad [pot?] of coffee the one [he pantomimes pouring] on top of the fire. The first thing you do is [roast] ya … roast it, green beans of coffee.

So when the fire is on, you have the, what do you call it? [He pantomimes shuffling something horizontally in the air. I try and guess what this tool is called.] Then you put the green beans on the roaster handle. Long. Has a little … half size of cup but has a long stick so your hand not in the fire but you shake it, to roast. Then when roast it there's a smoke from roast coffee. You go around people who are drink coffee. Each person you go to people to smell it first. The smoke. Respect. The women is respect those who served coffee. People who gonna drink the coffee. Repect to people. She get up out of her chair and she go one person. To smell smoke. And the people they give her well respect for doing that.

Once she done with long thing [at this point we pull out our phones and do a search on the Internet to see what this tool is called. It looks like a dished ladle, with a long, thin handle capable of supporting the beans while being held over a fire. Not finding an official name for it, we decide to call it a coffee ladle]. She done with coffee ladle and … uh she have to put water in the pad. [Pad? I ask. No, with a "t" he says a bit frustrated. I still don't know what this is but encourage him to go on with his story as I type furiously on my laptop.] Pat. The … fill it up, the pat with water and put it on the fire. Awhile she ground the roasted coffee. [He thinks and begins again.]

While she ground roasted coffee, the pad fill it up by the water and she put it on the fire. I mean its boiling there. So they ground the coffee beans, roasted coffee beans and what you call a con-tai-ner made out of wood. It has very deep and they put the coffee roast in the circle deep of the wood. And they have a handle of wood and they dig it. [Pound? Grind? I don't want to interrupt him again.] You know what I mean? Like hammering. From top to bottom. Then after a while, they check. The ground coffee is you know. Right. Ya. Proper ground it. What you call it, the little [snaps finger to remember]. Made up from trees [Mat? I offer.] They put it there. Then they twist mat [he makes fold-over motion]. Wrap, this way, [he picks up a one dollar bill from our coffee table and folds it so that it resembles a funnel or chute. I see now that the hot, roasted beans need to be directed into the small mouth of a coffee pot]. One is the ground coffee inside. Keep shaking pad. Keep sitting in fire like [he points to me, making a connection with my favorite way to prepare coffee] cowboy style. They boil it 10 to 15 minutes.

Pad sit 10-15 minutes is ready. You can tell it's going to puff up overflow. And so, the lady she watching there to make sure not falling all coffee out of pad. [She catches the overflow in a small container and returns it to the pot]. She see that sign. The woman she has to take out of the fire and have to put proper made out of, by same thing.

We digress as I confirm that pad and pat are meant to be "pot". I try to teach him the correct pronunciation. We practice as I exaggerate the sounds and movements of my mouth. A couple of people turn to look at us causing us to laugh good naturedly.

> After a while it ready. She have to take it out of fire. And let it sit. And ya, you using different something to eat that go with that coffee like some bread or pop corn uh or some biscotti. She serve all the food first. She start … what you call it? [Coffee or demitasse cup?], and ya, serve the people.
>
> Oh ya some people like a little spicy like ground ginger in their coffee. And some people they like it mix the coffee with cream or milk. But 90 % populate drink straight coffee.
>
> And the woman, she keep … I think a coffee box. Everything you need to make it, you put there. So you don't have to look item every day. Packed together. When you trying making coffee locked there. Closed. It has wheels too. You can push. Woman have little chair made out of wood. You can buy it everywhere you go. You can bought it in shop from Eritrea. Ethiopian. They bring it from back home. Make it more stylish. You know how many times we drink? We drink coffee three times.
>
> First level you serve everyone. Is it strong coffee. You serve them the first one, I'm sure, the pot is empty. [I smile.] Boil water and put it back in the fire, then 10 minutes later, I mean it's ready. You serve them again. The third last one, because the coffee getting thick, I mean thin. They add more coffee ground and add it on top … to make coffee stronger. Then they put back in fire. Then after 10 minutes they serve the third one. So …
>
> … at the end all the people who got served coffee they

86

just appreciate. Respect. Say thank you. The woman
wash, wash all the coffee cups, the pad. I mean pot.
Ready for next time. Morning and afternoon. Anytime
for special time.

About 14-15 so, a woman starts. Sure she will make
mistakes first or second time but after that she I know
everything in order. It's all about the ...

And so, Robel included the coffee ritual to his café' in the
squat. His customers appreciated the familiarity in the foreign
land. Business was booming. Then the pressure of all the new
arrivals began to take their toll on the different communities
living together.

So many people! All different country. We have
problems with Moroccans. Reason we have conflict
because they don't spend, pretty much ... A lot time in
squat, they just come, sleep. They spend that in the city
Rome. Doing business or whatever. Drunk somewhere
in ... in middle of night. Two o'clock in morning. Coming
out of nightclub. Drink at bar. They come in drunk,
make noise us all the time. Fighting each other. Pretty
much, every night.

One time they get ... they bit. One Arab bit one of
Eritrean guys. He was swollen. His face, everythings.
Next morning we come together to, what we have to do
about him. We set a meeting and we planning rid of
them. From *that,* squat. Because we was large number,
more than their number. How we gonna rid them? We
kicked them out at night; we wake them up at five in
morning. While they keep sleep. We kicked them out.
They scary. They never come back after that.

More and more people coming sea. We meet Sinistra
and they helping us a bigger place. And that's where
after this, we move. About 100 from first squat moved
to second. Organized other people from small squat or

living in house that have kids. When we go second squat, other people nationality don't go. We all Eritrean and Ethiopian going to second.

COLATINA ZONE: SQUAT NUMBER TWO

On the appointed day, members of the Sinistra political party brought a bus to pick up 150-200 people and take them to an abandoned government building. More ethnic groups joined: Sudanese, Ethiopians, Moroccans, Tunisians, Bangladeshis, Palestinians, women, children, and lots of families. Together, they busted the doors open and occupied the building.

"What's in it for the Sinistra?," I asked. Media and publicity, he told me as he was sipping his coffee.

The building in the Colatina zone was seven stories high. It had water leaking in from underground, mold, and flooding everywhere, but, "It was *seven* level high." Waving his arms in the air, Robel emphasized the *possibilities*. Word spread, and more people arrived until the ranks of the homeless swelled to over 300.

> Everyone have rooms, which used be offices. City of Rome, like city hall. Really high tech building. It was glass. Was uh, nice floor, lobby. They just scary because of flood and left.

> The police come. You have to protect yourself peacefully. For three hours, we keep building. Then we started sleeping and have watchers all night. Three-hour guard duty. Rotate. It like this for week. Police give up. There too many people. Too many media.

The main gate was located in the center of the rectangular architecture. It revealed an open hall with a ceiling. Robel lived on the third floor. I asked him what the floors looked like. (Gray. Tile.) Did the offices have open balconies? (No. But all the rooms had windows facing outside.) Office spaces? (Yes). Garbage Bins? (Yes, and the squatters hauled away the garbage.) What did it smell like? (Like a new office, but closed up.) What was his sleeping situation? (Robel found and brought in a metal-framed chair/bed convertible complete with mattress. It folded up into a chair for the day and folded out into a bed at night.) Did anyone have dogs or cats? (No.) Did you have to steal electricity? (No, it was already on.)

The ever-resourceful Robel quickly set up a small café just inside the front door, to the right in the lobby. Soon he hired a girl, and they both made coffee. Robel purchased and brought in the green coffee beans, and the girl roasted them in a pan over a small, camping-sized, electric stove. Again, the coffee was brewed in a traditional Eritrean clay pot. A little fabric filter is used to prevent the grounds from pouring out of the spout as the coffee is served in small demitasse cups. He sold the coffee for the equivalent of 50¢.

The café became even more popular when he added a billiard table, and people played a game similar to bocce ball using the pool balls and their hands. Next he bought a soccer table game.

Robel decided to expand into making breakfast: eggs, mashed potatoes, sausage, bacon, wraps, and toasted French bread. Every morning, he took his bike and bought fresh bread from a local bakery.

For lunch, Robel's café began serving cold beer, Pepsi, and other drinks. Soon two more "ladies" and one man were hired to keep up. "My place getting busy busy busy!" Robel was still only 24 years old.

Just as things were getting more comfortable the city of Rome cut off the electricity.

Robel remembered that about half of the squatters came out and blocked the main road; they sat down in the road to protest. The media returned. So did the police.

They talking us. The mayor of Rome arrive us and tell that he turn it back on, and city picks up bill. We now have legal free water and electricity. He signed papers in front of everyone.

The mayor also changed the status of the former abandoned government building to a residency building. "Everyone went home. Everythings open up. Everyone feel safer and live in open."

Robel's squatter's café expanded even further as a result of the confidence everyone felt, plus the promise of plentiful water and electricity. He was now open until two in the morning. A boom box provided loud pop music from various places: Sudanese, Eritrean, Amharic, Arabic, British and sometimes American. They would change it to suit the different customers.

Two competitors sprung up, but Robel had chosen the best spot in the building, right by the front door. It was the social meeting hub, and everyone had to pass it to come and go. With the money that he made, Robel helped his parents in Eritrea. He also used €8,000 (sent with people he trusted and community networking) to bring his brother in from Sudan. His brother traced the familiar route: Libya, "then float by sea to Italy," and continue on land. With no rent and no electrical costs for Robel. "It was all good." Robel lived like this for four years.

ROME, ITALY CONTINUED
Interview: 9:54 a.m., April 15, 2013, Strawberry Starbucks, Mill Valley, CA

Robel was restless in Italy. It was, "No right place to stay. No good documents. No guarantee documents because they renew every year."

He continued …

> Don't want to stay in Italy. Not good plan. Plan go to United Kingdom. But once fingerprinted in Italy, you get [turned away in other countries]. Italy is now forever your home. You can stay but not working. Italy has agreement with European Economic Community. My new plan going United States or Canada because they don't have agreement. I fingerprinted there.

The money he'd saved at the squatter's café helped broker his brother out of Eritrea and into Germany via the same Italian refugee camp where he had been. He warned his brother to escape the camp in Lampadusa *before* he was fingerprinted.

Out of 250 people, five ran away, including his brother. "They climbing tall wall." Robel stood up in our coffee shop and pantomimed the height. The wall at the camp was 6-8 feet high. His brother successfully made his way to Germany, and it became his official port of entry.

Robel worked his café for about four years. More and more people arrived daily as Robel was planning to move on. He dedicated himself to saving money, doing his research via networking, and waiting for the right time.

"What did you do with your coffee shop?" I asked. "I give some family member. Not a lot money, but …"

The new plan had the following parameters: Using his refugee status, Robel was able to travel throughout Europe, everywhere except the United Kingdom. The first stop on his transatlantic passage would be France.

Robel's brother had a secure job in Germany and was able to add cash to what Robel had saved. The value of the euro would go further in developing countries than in Europe, so transportation tickets would be bought en route. A *pay-as-you-go* strategy would also allow flexibility in time.

Through the networking web of refugees and Eritrean community, Robel collected contact information for brokers, drivers, guides, safe houses, and homes. He also gleaned tips on survival, safety, customs and anything to help him cross borders without being killed, extorted, captured, and turned into indentured servitude (or slavery), or simply thrown into prison or deported. He told me stories that circulated about migrants getting caught up in human trafficking and organ harvesting. These are some of the fears that Robel thought about at night.

FRANCE

Location: Paris, France
Interview: 9:18 a.m., May 8, 2013, Strawberry Starbucks, Mill Valley, CA

Robel had one travel companion for the next leg of his journey. They flew to Paris together, bringing only their carry-on bags. At arrival, they easily and quickly found signs for the taxi stand. The cab driver spoke Italian and French. They asked him to take them to the cheapest, most affordable hotel.

From the hotel, it was four or five miles to the Cuban Embassy. They used public transportation to get there.

I stopped Robel, "Perhaps this is a stupid question, but in your mind, did you think that maybe this is the only time in your life that you will ever be in Paris? Did you want to see something while you were there?"

His face lit up as he spilled out the few tourist sites they were able to visit in the brief three days. "Leonardo da Vinci's Mona Lisa, The Metropolitan is … ya, amazing. Big! Go to it from Underground. We also went all the way to top of…" he made a triangle with his fingertips together. "Eiffel Tower?" I asked. "Yes! It was so beautiful at night." His white teeth glistened as he smiled.

I explained the concept of culture shock.

> I mean, it wasn't culture shock to me because I was in Italy, almost five years. But uh, they have pretty much similar, tasty food. When you eat some bakery and salmon sandwich. I just … I like way they cook. We was so very, like, occupied to go to our free. More paying attention, mission is how to get out of *that* country … go

next one. The French coffee different from Italian too. Cappuccino in France, I like better. Because flavor, mocha thing, they add it in there.

The Cuban Embassy wanted them to return the next day to finish their paperwork. They got permission on the third day. Then, to a travel agency, to purchase their plane ticket to Cuba.

THE CARRIBEAN

CUBA

Location: Havana, Cuba

Their stay in Havana lasted one week. After arriving around nine-thirty at night, they walked out of the "very big" airport and were greeted by hot and humid air plus crowds of people and taxis vying for riders. Robel spoke little Spanish, but they managed to find a cab driver who knew of a safe and cheap hotel.

Their hotel stay was simple and relaxed: "shower, eating restaurant bar." Both slept well. Both had "a really big feeling," he told me with a sparkle in his eyes.

On the first morning, they called their connection in Honduras … "or was it Panama? I don't speak Spanish."

They wanted to let their connection know they'd arrived in Cuba as planned. They gave him their contact information, hotel and room number, so the smuggler could call them back, because it was so expensive to call out from the hotel. The smuggler spoke English, which made it less difficult to communicate. Arrangements were made.

"We stay in. Very strict. Limited," he makes chopping motions on our table.

"Hey, I have a question," I began. "How is it that you knew any English?"

> Oh, ya, we learn in school. A little English. A little Arabic. Hear a little Tigrinya. Ya … my father, he sell things [merchant].

I hopped on the Internet later that day to do a little research. As with the United States, there is no official language of Eritrea. Turns out that Eritrea has many languages. Nine to be exact. The top three, used mostly for business and commerce, are Tigrinia (approximatly 50% of the population uses this) plus Arabic and English. Other prevelant languages include: Tigre (40%), Afar (4%), Saho (3%), Bega (or Beja), Bilen, Nara, and Kunama. Because Mussolini's government used Eritrea as a base to conquer and colonize Ethiopia (in the 1930s), many Eritreans were also exposed to the Italian language.

CENTRAL AMERICA

PANAMA

Location: Unknown

The Eritrean friends were given two tickets to an airport somewhere in Panama. They arrived around 6:00 p.m. without incident. I asked Robel how the contacts found them at the busy airport and he chuckled, "How we look, and time was right."

Two men spotted them. One spoke English. I asked Robel to describe them, his first impressions. They wore tennis shoes, designer jeans, T-shirts, and dark sunglasses. They kept glancing around. Neither smiled. I explained to Robel what the euphemism *shady-looking characters* means and he said *yes*, that was them, *precisely*. The Eritreans followed them.

The drive was about 30 minutes long and ended at a two-bedroom house on the outskirts of a city. Once in, they were offered water. About 15 other Latinos were already there and appeared to have been rounded up from all over. Peru? Brazil? Argentina? Robel and his friend were the only Africans. Spanish and Portuguese (it seemed to him) were the most common languages spoken.

"Everyone looked tired. Maybe some of them walked?" Robel imagined. There were three- or four-year old children crying, women, families, single people, and young adults who looked around 17 years old.

The house was nestled between mountains; tall trees and a huge back yard surrounded it. The sky was overcast.

Robel and his friend were more tired than nervous. They spent one night sleeping on the carpeted floor. Everyone had to be ready at 5:00 a.m.. A van arrived, and the professional smugglers hissed, "*Salida! Rápido! Rápido!*," -as everyone, with their few belongings, scurried to get into a van.

Each person paid the shady pair of men $500 for this leg of the trip.

COSTA RICA

Location: Unknown

The drivers swapped off as they careened through the night. Robel described them as "driving like crazy" and "so very rushed."

"Bam, bam, many holes." They avoided main roads. Everything was hills, mountains, and local tracts of land. "Where we going, where we end up, we did not know. No windows in van."

At this point in the story, Robel and I segued into a discussion on what we, in American vernacular, call a *serial killer van*. I asked him if he felt helpless or afraid. He was more concerned about getting arrested and deported than getting murdered.

The ride had been so stressful that many of the women and children were crying. They wanted to get out.

To keep a low profile, the drivers made only one, one-hour stop at a gas station. It was part of the human highway network, and their arrival was expected. The drivers hung out with the employees, stretched their legs, and chatted amicably as everyone went to the bathroom, filled their water containers and helped themselves to "free" food. "Like tamales things. They sell from truck in front of gas station."

Robel only knew that they were somewhere deep in mountains. After the one-hour break ended, everyone was hustled back into the van. On the positive side, the van *was* air-conditioned. Some time around 2:00 a.m. they stopped and the migrant smugglers announced, "We're here."

The Eritreans had no idea where, in Costa Rica, *here* was. "We don't know we in Costa Rica. Maayyybeeee at end, we know."

NICARAGUA

Location: Unknown

It was the same scenario. "There are limits to where stopping," Robel taps, "this, this, this," his fingers illustrate a journey across our coffee table. "Still we have to travel."

Another truck stop that offered lots of bath- and shower rooms, stocked with towels and soap. The restaurant provided simple, local food for purchase. Robel and his traveling companion had to buy their own tamales. The showers were free.

The landscape surrounding the truck stop was nondescript dirt, with patches of trees here and there. Everyone dozed in plastic backyard chairs. The only sounds were flies buzzing around, and a generator played in the background: *bop, bop, bop*. There was nothing else but hot air.

At 6:00 p.m. everyone was ushered back into the windowless van. They drove the entire next day. "Seems to me like eight at night, we stop at ... [creek]. Just stopping... there at water. A lot of trees." Robel compared them to the trees at Muir Woods here in Marin County. He opened his arms wide and peered up saying, "Very, very thick, tall trees."

> We take break under trees. Eating food from truck stop. Very hot. Dry. Staying about one hour. Just rest. They say us ... everyone quiet. No talking. Back into van. No benches. No seats ... in van. Keep driving, driving, driving.

It took approximately two days and nights to arrive at Nicaragua sometime around 11:00 p.m.

It was a huge "rich person fancy house" with lots of rooms. There was a "nice garden with lot of fruit (orange, coconut, apple, mango) and very nice bathrooms." He raised his eyebrows and showed his bright teeth as he smiled. Robel knew he was in Nicaragua because of the magazines and newspapers lying about.

Food was brought in for the travelers: tamales, bread, and mandarin juice in a glass bottle. "You know they make a lot of money. I believe it was owner and his family, the big boss. Not person who driving us, but house owner."

They waited all day to see what the next step was. Everyone was given an option: to fly or ride to El Salvador. "We and three other people want fly, ya. One from Ecuador, one from Peru, and one ... maayyybeeee from Brazil."

Robel was in the group of five who took a taxi to the airport. The rest left in vans. The mood was more relaxed.

I stopped Robel right there. "How is it that you could just get on a plane? What about documents? Passports? Tickets?"

He backtracked to when he'd arrived in Panama. Robel and his friend had paid $300 each, to have the arrangements made. Everything that they needed, including traveling by plane, was waiting for them at this house. He surmised that airport workers were paid not to scrutinize the documents too closely.

Robel and his friend only carried two daypacks, which helped simplify the process and speed at which they went through the various airport security and checkpoints. They were also split up, so each went through the airport alone and sat alone on the plane. In this way, there wouldn't be any conversation that might alert someone. And, obviously, if one person were detained, the others would be able to carry on as if they weren't involved. The plane left for El Salvador around 4:00 p.m.

EL SALVADOR

Location: Unknown

There was one cab driver waiting in the airport for people getting off the plane. "We easy found. We the only two black Africans."

The other three travelers joined them. The cab driver asked the Ecuadorian in the group questions to confirm their identity, and then, *"go, go, go* quickly to his taxi." All five got in, and they were taken to a motel in a city. It had two floors and roughly seven to ten rooms. "Not fancy. Just for sleep. Two in room. Maybe one by his self."

"Ya, just take shower and waiting. The room smelled *"bad!"* Robel's makes a sour face and shakes his head as if flinging off an offensive liquid.

> Like something growing. Me and my friend, we don't sleep. Smelled moldy. Maybe marijuana. Bed not so clean either. We don't eat breakfast. It was around seven. We waiting. The travel to Guatemala was supposed be flight but they cancel, ya. Maybe they don't have connection. Then we waiting, waiting, waiting. Worst place ever. Reservations locked up? Maybe connection at airport get caught. Who knows? They don't make it.

They went to the coffee shop directly across the street. "Can't go far. Maybe police catch you." They lived on burritos, tacos with rice, and different kinds of soft drinks. I asked Robel how he was able to keep paying for these unexpected mishaps: food, pay phones, delays.

When he'd been in Cuba, money came to him from Italy via Western Union. His brother (whom he helped travel from Eritrea to Germany) was now, in turn, helping him. He held Robel's money and also dipped into his own pockets, when needed. More money was sent to Robel while he was in Panama as well.

The motel had an ancient television with an antenna on top and Spanish-only channels. Neither slept much at night, maybe two, three or four hours. Sometimes, Robel recalled, he would sleep, wake, peek out of the curtains only to be disappointed that it was still the same day. Time dragged. Nothing changed.

They were stuck on the outskirts of a small town. Robel was no longer sure of the name, but he sounded out some possibilities: "Koute Begae or CoJute Peke, or Cojutepeque?" We were not able to find it (or most of the other stepping stones of his trek) on a map.

Looking at some magazines and newspapers at the coffee shop across the street, Robel was able to find bits of English and get a glimpse of what was going on in the world. There were also the coffee shop regulars, some of whom they were able to communicate a little with. Gleaning bits and pieces, the Africans were able to surmise that they were trapped in a particularly dangerous town, and the sounds they heard, both day and night, were indeed gunshots. Drugs, murders, robbery, street fights; it was enough to keep them in their smelly room where time stood still.

Robel began anticipating the sliver of sunlight that worked its way between the curtains and across the moldy, airless room.

Eventually, there was a meeting between the brokers and foreigners. The possibility of a flight to Guatemala had been foiled. They had been waiting for the airport circumstances to change, but it was probably not going to happen soon. The airport would eventually be secure when some people got caught. The smugglers presented two options: Whoever wanted to, could wait indefinitely until it was safe to use the airport, again or … they could go by land. More specifically, travel with an 18-wheeler truck, which meant they would most likely have to ride in the back and in the heat. "You really want to go? Go by truck," they said.

One hot and still day, a car arrived at the motel to transport them to where a semi-tractor trailer was waiting. The nearly vacant truck stop was 15 minutes away from the seedy motel. "We meet driver and have coffee with him and taking a little time to get to know each other. It felt very freer," Robel motioned towards his chest in a gesture of relief.

The trucker trained them on what to do. They were to hide between the pallets in the middle, in the back. He knew exactly where all the checkpoints were and what the procedure was. The inspectors never pulled things out but just looked and concentrated on the paperwork to make sure it was in order. "He say, 'As long as they have paperwork, who care?'" Robel had the impression that the driver was in his 40s and very experienced. His family was from Uruguay, but he was born and raised in Guatemala.

The truck cabin had room for a driver and a passenger. Directly behind the seats was a space for the driver to bed down and sleep. The truck was equipped with a new television and electronics. Robel rode up front first, while his friend relaxed in the bed.

> Maybe we did, like, five times checkpoints. Not too strict. Twice times we hide in cab bed, standing in corners. I very nervous, but you know, you say yourself, no problem. No problem.

> Four days I think, and five nights. We stop for eating at truck stops. Shower there. Stretch legs. Watch TV at truck stops. Maybe we help him out, change bad tire. Very, very nice guy. He pay us sometimes food. We

listen Spanish music, soccer news on radio. We driving to some big city in Guatemala, I don't know.

GUATEMALA

Location: Unknown
Interview: 10:00 a.m., June 24, 2013, Peet's Coffee, Novato, CA

When Robel and I met again at Peet's for our coffee, interview, and note-taking session, he recapped the 18-wheeler story. The driver had been very curious about Africa. The three men got along amicably.

This latest human smuggling transport had begun in El Salvador and continued through Guatemala. They hid in the back of the noisy 18-wheeler and Robel admitted, this time, to being very nervous. He was always shaky about getting caught. The already hot interior of the container seemed to spike with the sound of the inspectors voices, right before they opened up the back to poke around.

The nauseating exhaust fumes added to the stress. Robel suffered intense migraines.

I asked Robel what would happen if they were caught. He would tell them he was from Ethiopia rather than Eritrea. The country of Ethiopia would release him, because they know the political situation. I asked him to elaborate some more on this.

> Military with no end. No pay. Just pocket money. Can't support family. Maayyybeeee you see family one time in year, if you are lucky. I know somebodies who are *still* in Eritrean Army, for 15 years. You can't leave.

To gain more insight, I went to the Human Rights Watch online and found a page that referred to the army experience as service for life: Usually prompted by an arbitrary arrest or detention. In most cases this type of situation would evolve into torture, forced labor, and usually prison. Another part of the Human Rights Watch site included details of a myriad of prisons. The descriptions were in line with his stories.

At this point in his travels, he told me, he wasn't so much afraid for his life, but afraid for all the time, trouble, and money lost.

Robel and his friend would often ride for four or five hours straight, in the back with the cargo. When the situation was right, the driver would "pull over on emergency road, like he checking tires, then boom, boom, boom, let us out for a break and back into cab."

Robel described a little hole in the side and bottom of the container, "made for leaking out water. That's your air. Your only fresh air." Otherwise, they would nestle between boxes and pallets. Make a little space for themselves in the middle.

I asked him how he passed the time.

> Always thinking. Stopped talking friend. Long, long journey. Friend say 'too much hot,' and he thinking we die from heat. Friend say he don't care and wanted to go, uh, up front. Even if he caught. He can't resist anymore. "I...," Robel said proudly, "have resistance for everythings! Have to pass a lot of problems for better life."

Once they reached Guatemala, it was mostly highway. "Always hot. Sometimes we stop every three maayyybeeee four hours. Make phone calls. Eat food. Take showers. He on phone, say person on the Mexican border who going help us."

Robel and his friend rotated between the cab and bed when it was safe to ride up front in air-conditioning. They saw Guatemalan people selling food (corn, tamales, burritos, mandarin soft drinks, oranges, mangos, grapes, apples) on the side of truck stops. "They very poverty."

The nights were hot and humid, but not "too bad."

NORTH AMERICA

MEXICO

"The river is the border," he was told.

"Was it the Suchiate river?" I asked Robel. I had been doing some research, and that seemed like a popular place for crossing into Mexico.

"Who remembers name? The mission is only get there…"

The 18-wheeler reached its destination around 6:00 p.m. A river guide was expecting them, waiting in his dilapidated pickup at a truck stop.

"Hi, my name is Emmanuel," and from there, the guide drove them to his "very nice home" and treated the Africans like guests. Emmanuel introduced them to his wife and two children. Robel and his friend took showers, ate dinner, and shared one bedroom, with two beds, that night. They both slept fully and woke refreshed the next day.

A small shopping trip was made with Emmanuel to buy blue bed sheets and new shirts. This caught my attention and I stopped the story. Blue? Why blue, I wondered. Was it some sort of special camouflage? Was it a signal to someone? Robel said there was no particular reason. It was the only color they had.

At around 6:00 p.m., they left on foot to make their way through a forest. When they reached the river, about 30 minutes later, Emmanuel gave them bright orange life vests and shorts to wear in the water. Wallets went into pants' pockets, and the pants (along with their shoes) were wrapped around their necks. They had to abandon their daypacks.

In the light from the setting sun, they saw that the river was formidable in its strength. They would have to cross barefooted for less drag and a better grip.

Emmanuel knew exactly where to step and how to work his way diagonally against the current. The travelers held fast to him and each other, with both hands, and "walked like an Egyptian." Robel was really, really scared. The current was so strong that, several times, it threatened to knock them off their feet and sweep them downstream to their death. Sometimes they would step into holes. Sometimes the river bottom would rise up, revealing a submerged sand bar. Sometimes they were waist deep in water. It was a roaring, noisy, muddy river. It was dirty too, but not "too stinky." Robel estimated that it was about 60-70 feet wide.

The river's edge was lined with rocks, and if you broke free of the Egyptian hand hold, you would be smashed with force into them. They went slowly, calculating and testing every single step. It took them 20 minutes to cross, but Robel said it was like a lifetime.

The two Africans and their guide climbed out of the river basin, over the rocks onto flat ground, and changed into their dry clothes and new shirts. It was hot, even though the sun had set.

Emmanuel took them to some small, abandoned houses. They had thatched roofs and were probably used for the agricultural workers to take refuge from the hot sun when working the fields. The land was filled with mango, mandarin and orange trees. In the dying light, they could make out a fertile countryside. That night, they spread their new, light-blue bed linens on the floor of a small, old hut and slept in them.

> When sun raising up, we waking up. The water [canal] goes garden [agricultural field]. We follow and wash faces. Not really clean water, but you gottta wash your face. We walking by water with guide, through gardens so no one can see us. We arriving at a camp named Tapa Sheela [spelled phonetically; could it be Tapachula migration station?] around 11 in morning.

Emmanuel stopped within sight of the camp and said, "Bye-bye, done my job, good luck," and pointed towards the compound.

Staring at the compound, they knew they would be *analyzed* and perhaps sent back. They knew that, whether they walked in or kept traveling by foot, they might get caught and deported. Either way. The two friends took a deep breath and walked up to a guard in an army-green Mexican government uniform. They, were admitted.

A MIGRATION STATION
Location: Unknown

At this point in Robel's story, I turned to the Internet again and read more on these types of migration camps to understand why anyone would risk turning themselves in rather than forging forward on his or her own. The answer was simple: It was ultimatly safer.

Many of the migrants who travel through Mexico inevitably end up on some of the same routes as organized criminals, since both of them shared the goal of avoiding detection. Some of the migrants inevitably ran into crooks who figured out ways to take advantage of them (extortion, human trafficing, sex slaves, "mules," gangs, kidnapped women and children, forced prostitution, etc.). Many of the Mexican routes move Colombian cocaine to the north, which adds a level of dangerous weaponary to the mix. Plus, migrants (who are often easy to spot because of their ethnicity) carry cash, but rarely anything more lethal than a knife. So by handing yourself over to official migration stations, you are somewhat lessening the perils of the underworld routes.

It was a huge camp surrounded by barbed wire, seven or eight feet high. The buildings were made of cement. The compound contained offices, rooms with beds, a dining room, showers, a basketball court, and a place for "TV watching". Wooden and plastic furniture was scattered everywhere.

Robel explained why he felt confident:

> The people that helping us, know it is safe place for Eritreans. It is a business. It *has* to be successful. They want do best they can. It's money. They want *more* people. So ... ya, that's how they do it.

119

Officially, in theory at least, Mexico's immigration policy is driven by human rights concerns. However, a serious flaw in the process is that the Mexican officials do not speak Eritrean, nor are the official documents written in Eritrean. Even if the immigrants were not deported but released instead, the legal documents that define them or are handed to them can cause a lot of confusion. With no one to translate, the legal parameters spelled out in them (for example whether you are allowed to travel or work, where you can live, expiration dates, mandatory return dates, etc.) could have disastrous results if misinterpreted or not adhered to.

> In camp, ya ... people from all different country, we saw a lot people deport [he snaps his fingers], every day they get deport. A lot of people coming. A lot of people going. Some people come and go in same day! Depend on situation. But some stay.

"Basically," Robel said, "it was like prison. Like immigration on hold." First they were strip-searched. Next all their personal possessions, including money, were put into clear plastic bags and stored up on a shelf. Robel said you had to remember which bag was yours. They confiscated shoe laces "in case you gonna suicide."

Then came the interviewer. "They don't really care how you getting there. They do care *'why you here.'"*

Robel continued, "I have a problem in my country. I run away from government. If I go back I get arrest or killed. I just say them straight, I don't wanna go back."

The Mexican official said, "We help you. We give you a house. Papers."

But the Africans said, "We don't want any problems. We just want go. Just leave. We don't want a house or papers."

"Tapa Sheela" contained five Eritreans, two Somalis, and about 15 Africans from other countries. Robel and his friend met people from all corners of the world. There were also lots of Latin Americans.

> We probably travel longest because we from East Africa and crossing land. One Eritrean woman travel with her boyfriend to Kenya, then straight Mexico. Other woman, who alone, she went South Africa, then Guatemala, then Mexico.

I asked how the women were dressed.

> You must march with the people of land you in. Both womans wore western. You wear traditional clothes, you highlight. You get caught. Sent back. Maybe killed by your government.

At the camp, everyone received soap, a blanket, a bed, a room, and a breakfast-lunch-dinner schedule. There were three levels of bunk beds with six people per room. Two Africans [Robel wasn't sure what country they were from], two Somalis, Robel, and his friend.

To pass the time, the refugees watched television, played basketball, took showers, and browsed Spanish magazines. They were locked in every night where they would "hang out and waiting; what they will do with us."

The food was pocessed and of poor quality. They ate cereal, tamales, beans, rice, eggs, and Jell-O, and drank tea.

> Waiting find out decision. One day, man come in. Call name. Ready go. Where? Not know. Give our stuff back. 'Taking you to Mexico City camp.' About twelve of us into van. We can't get out. Some bread and water. We driving 12 hours straight. No stopping! It was on a fast, fast highway [interstate].

The terrain was mostly flat, without much to distract the passengers. Nothing to do but sleep, make light conversation or just sit quietly. The van had one driver and two officers with machine guns (possibly Kalashnikovs) in the back with everyone. The passengers were treated with respect. The guards were "just doing their jobs."

When they arrived, it was the same type of camp, designed like a compound with cells, to hold refugees, illegal aliens, and those seeking political asylum. They passed through the gates.

Location: Mexico City, Mexico
Interview: 9:58 a.m., July 8, 2013, Peet's Coffee, Mill Valley, CA

> In the Mexico City the military waiting us. They open [detention center] gate to compound. They taking six people out driving side to office and six people right side to other office. Same thing, name, where you come from. Why you here.

Robel told me that they didn't want to hear you say that you intended to make your way to the United States or Canada. He'd heard that they prefer you request Mexico because "they get profit if you stay, from United Nations. As refugee, we need help, and United Nation gives you money. Maybe $2,000 per person. Mexico gives $500 to me and they keeping rest."

Another reason that Robel didn't want to stay in Mexico is that he believed it wasn't safe.

> They know where everyone is really trying go. The less we say them, the less blocks they put you up. I always think: What's going to happen? Always nervous. Maybe they deport me. Maybe they jail me. Always thinking. Thinking.

Again the same, "immigration holding. Like a jail." They took everything the travelers had: wallets, money, belts, shoelaces, wedding rings, etc. Three bunk beds per cell, with six people per cement room. He lived there approximately six weeks.

The problem with the food was that it was the same exact thing every day and the quality was questionable. For breakfast they had cereal, milk, hot tea, bagels, cream cheese, and bread. Lunch consisted of rice, soy sauce, beans and, corn on the cob. Sometimes bananas and apples. Dinner was rice, lentils, sometimes beef. Water in plastic bottles. Each day:

> There was sleep, wake up. Walk around camp. Small soccer. Take shower. One TV, in Spanish, for everyone. No books. No magazine. Outside can call in. You give them your phone number. No credit to make calls. Very expensive. Police always answers phone. In room by seven-thirty at night. Each block has own lock.

Roughly two weeks into the stay, the food had become so intolerable that it added to the anxiety and monotony of waiting. Robel just wanted to get out. He told the officials that he wanted to leave,

> No way. Boom! Boom! More interviews. Fingerprints. Process takes time. They taking pictures for files.

Robel and several others decided to engage in a hunger strike.

> The boss officer for compound explain us, it take one month. Then we decide. Who to go where and who to stay here.

They began to eat again.

> Then uh, after, you know, same thing. Day. Night. Get up. Sleep. Get up. Sleep. Waiting. Waiting. No plan except come United States and not get caught in Mexico. One thing we know ... it will take time but, ya, they will leave you ...

> More than one interview. Lots in one day. They asked if you wanna stay Mexico. Afford you home, money pocket, some food [he paused and thought a minute], like food stamps. I deny because Mexico is pretty much the same thing we left in Eritrea. I don't need anything except peace. They asked, 'What you want?' I say them,

'Just go free. Leave me alone. I don't need any help from Mexican government.'

When I got to Italy, I saw this is not good place to live. When I got to Mexico, I think same thing. Canada or USA. I can never go back to Africa. Go far. As far from Europe or Africa. Life in Italy struggling. Learn through friends there is opportunity in USA & Canada. England, Germany, Great Britain, they all send me back to Italy. And Italy not allow me work.

Just leave me alone.

So ya. After … one month arrived finally. They call us for six people leaving compound. We get white piece of paper [permit] for one month. After one month, you must be out of Mexico. When it expires, they take us jail.

Robel, his friend, two Eritrean men and women all declined. None wanted to stay in Mexico. All six were processed and released at once. Within their group were also two Ethiopians and two Somalis.

We have connection to cheap hotel in Mexico City that will let us stay with just paper. We don't have IDs. We taxi hotel together. Stay at hotel for two weeks. A lot of people pass through this hotel, so it's not unusual.

Family send money. We all need money crossing border. We give hotel owner's name to receive Western Union. She gets some of money, benefitted from having people stay at hotel. She don't ask questions.

At the cheap hotel, everyone had their own room. They hung out together, ate together, and figured out how to get out of Mexico City together. Everyone used their personal connections to network contacts and figure out how to get to the United States. Mexico City was the last stop. *The end of the plan.* "We don't know what next."

Connections had been arranged well ahead of time, before they even crossed into Mexico or any other border. Refugees who had gone before learned the process and shared their knowledge by lending hands to those behind them. Like a human chain, holding on to each other, they shared information by word of mouth to stay safe and keep from stumbling as they made their way towards a better life and distant lands of opportunity. And so was Robel, networking and helping others the whole time he journeyed.

I asked Robel how Yodit made her way to Marin County to join him. Surely, as a young woman alone, she didn't follow his same foot tracks?

Yodit traveled from Sudan to Ethiopia, Germany, and then the United States.

THE MAN FROM NIGERIA
Location: Unknown. Maybe Reynosa, Mexico

Robel received advice and contact information from a friend who was already living in the United States and who had arrived through a different network. The Nigerian, based in Mexico, helped people cross borders and wanted to meet Robel in person. He came to the hotel, and they went out for coffee at a café nearby. The meeting was like an interview and, at the end, Robel learned that the political asylum seekers would have to buy bus tickets to Reynosa (?), located on the Texas border.

For the first time during Robel's journey, he made it a point to document where he was. They took photos in front of a Mexican cab, complete with a Mexican flag in the background. He saved receipts: laundry tickets, grocery receipts, cab rides, basically everything that included a Mexican location and date. This was to prove that they were in Mexico and hadn't spent any time in the United States.

All six Eritreans boarded their bus early in the morning.

> We so close and we been so scary we going to get stopped and detained, even have our one-month permit. Nervous. Maybe government stops and say us, we can't go this way. The bus make bathroom and food stop. During stop, you called contact at border to let him know you coming. After 12 hours, we are in Reynosa. Maybe. Not sure name.
>
> Two people come in van. They pick us up at bus stop. We went motel with lot of rooms and lot people. They bring us food from store. We stay there. Rested. Sleep. Two days. We still not pay. We have making sure we really get there! We don't get robbed.

They waiting more people. Latin Americans. Africans. Asians. Maybe 300 people. Men. Womans. Familia.

Then they come us and say, 'We are going tonight. Have money ready. You have two options:

- Pay 500 US and we crossing border and river (maybe one 100 feet wide to crossing). After, you stay. Waiting. Maybe U.S. Border Patrol find you, then you good to go. Or...
- You pay 500 up front, then if you don't get caught, and you make it to Houston, *then* you pay 2,000 US.'

Robel opted for the second scenario because he wanted to apply as an asylum seeker, "in your own time, and with all documents prepared, hire attorney, ya."

If you chose the first option, anything could happen, Robel explained to me.

Maybe yes, maybe no. Maybe take forever. Maybe deport. Too risky. Too hard to do homework: research in US, ask people, find those [successfully] crossing. Analyzed. Find good lawyer references. You gotta know where to land before you jump.

All the people who had converged in the motel were separated according to those who were willing to get caught and those who were not. Roughly 25 people chose the second option, which involved travel by night.

They left around midnight and walked silently through a forest with three guides. One led the way up front, one was positioned on the side, and the third shepherding from behind. Each guide had a walkie-talkie. They made their way to a farm house.

They stayed at the house for one day. Without television, having to remain indoors and out of sight, Robel observed a steady stream of young people coming and going with sacks on their backs. He didn't know what was in the sacks (not backpacks), but it was BIG. Everyone was smoking marijuana freely and in the open.

"Were you nervous?" I asked again. "Ya, ya. Very scary. But have no choice." "Did anyone offer you marijuana?," I continued. "No, they know we deeply religious people and we don't do drugs."

It felt like a distribution point to Robel, as well as a resting place for the farmers.

THE RIVER IS THE BORDER
Interview: 9:44 a.m., August 14, 2013, Strawberry Starbucks, Mill Valley, CA

Robel had a new backpack, and it was filled with socks, a shirt, pants, and tennis shoes. Everything was bought in Mexico. He also carried bottled water, snacks, crackers, and chips.

Around 10:00 p.m. and under the cover of night, they started to walk amongst the trees and grass, guided by the three organizers with walkie-talkies again. Since they were at the border, they had to be very quiet. At one point, the border patrol trucks came near, and everyone dove under the trees. Sharp thorns pricked and drew blood as the searchlights swept the landscape around them.

"Rápido! Rápido!" They made their way to a river that was less than ¼ mile wide. It was too deep to cross without the inflatable plastic rafts that the *coyotaje* unfolded. Robel took a turn pumping the air into one. It did not appear to have multiple air chambers, so if it was punctured, the whole thing would sink. Each raft held five people, so they had to paddle back and forth seven or eight times to get everyone across.

The migrants sat silently in the sandy, prickly woods, waiting for the operation to complete. It took about an hour and a half.

On the other side of the river, they were on the other side of the border. They had made it to the United States.

The group walked in single file, sometimes with their hands on their heads. There was metal fencing everywhere, designed to keep the animals out of the crops. Robel recalls (while making tangled motions with his hands) that it was very difficult for the women to cross the wire fences "over and over." Their progress was slow but steady as night turned to dawn.

By six in the morning, they arrived at a family home where everyone rested for the day.

> They get paid. You know what I mean? We stay all long day. Rested until around four in afternoon and then have to get on brand new pickup truck, open air.

They were positioned head to foot and told to lie as flat as they could in the truck bed. Everyone was covered in woven fabric and stretched plastic. The driver "driving like crazy all over the road." Robel was certain that it was over 100 miles per hour. The grueling ride lasted three to four hours through Texas and ended when they were dropped off in a forest. It was night again.

> We start walking. Three guys leading us. Walked all night. *All* night. In daytime we stop. Rest under trees because helicopters around us. We hear everywhere. Food. Water. Walk again. Safer walk all night.

> Around six or seven in the morning, ya, uh, we keep walking … see a lot animals. Cows. Deer. Coyotes. Rabbits. The ladies getting tired. They want to stop. Rest. Four or five kids. They're bad. Have to carry them on backs. Keep traveling four days and nights from crossing river.

At one point, the coyotajes thought someone had spotted and reported them crossing a main road. Exhausted, the group ran and collapsed in the woods to hide for three or four hours. It began to rain a little at first and then to really pour. Everyone got wet, and then the cold set in. No one had prepared them for rain, and no one had rain gear. In between their teeth chattering, the women said they couldn't move any more. Energy depleted, the women cried, and everyone was spent. The smugglers called their contacts in Houston, Texas, and ordered two minivans. When they arrived, everyone piled in. They headed towards Houston, a couple of hours away.

Upon arrival, they were ushered into another house to hide. This one was empty. It had three or four bedrooms upstairs. The Eritreans (two women and four men) slept, splayed out on the carpet, from about eleven in the morning to six in the evening, all in one room.

UNITED STATES

Location: Houston, Texas
Interview: 9:51 a.m., on a Monday, Peet's Coffee, Mill Valley, CA

"After we get rest, we get phone. People hold us … give it to us." Most immigrants were able to leave the same day because they had the cash with them.

> One Eritrean from us have a family member living in Houston long time. They know he's coming. As soon as my friend called his family, they bring money same day. My friend explained him where we here. They meet outside. We stay in house. He picked up and went to Houston."

> We don't have money. I call my brother in Germany and give coyotajes guys name with right spelling. I say him *if* you miss one spelling, Western Union not give money. Should be same day, but it was Germany. I call at night but in Germany it's day shift. My brother call me back again. The coyotajes guys want Western Union code. Then I give it to them, because there's some 24-hour Western Union store, and they want cash-out money.

> Robel had ordered twice the fee amount from his brother, a total of $5,000. Half was for himself, the other half was for his friend. "You see," he explained, "we don't want them know my friend already has money. If they steal us, we still have cash. My friend pay me back. Later."

Once Robel gave the Mexicans the Western Union wire transfer code, they left in the early morning to pick up the money.

> You know what they say me? There's a missing number. They don't cash out money. "Oh really? Give me phone to call my brother." They say, "We don't have international phone credit left. Can't dial out."
>
> "'Lets go outside" they say me, "and buy another calling card and also some food for your friends."

"I went with them," Robel recalled looking down into his coffee.

> Three guys in one truck. They take me wherever we are going far, far from house. One spoke English. They keep asking. They keep investigating me; if I was in military. They keep asking me complicated questions. I know now they wanted know everythings I can do to them.

Sitting in our noisy café, I frowned into my coffee, trying to understand what Robel meant. Then I got it, "Oh! They were trying to figure out if you were a ninja warrior and you were going to kick their butts if they tried to mess with you, right?" Yes, he said, and we both chuckled.

At first, he thought the three Mexicans in the truck were just trying to be friendly. But the questions became more and more pointed. As soon as they figured out that he could defend himself, they changed their original plan, which was to isolate him, take his money in a *peaceful way,* as he put it, and dump him far from the house, then drive off. That way they could go back and report to their boss that they had a *runner* who disappeared with his fee. But now, they suspected he would use his military training to resist and fight them. Maybe one of them would get hurt. How would they explain that?

134

Instead, they took him to a crowded shopping mall that included the largest single store that Robel had ever seen. Today, he suspects it was one of those giant Walmart Supercenters that includes groceries as well as everything else.

Two of the Mexicans remained in the truck, across the street, parked under a bridge, and watched. The third accompanied Robel. As soon as they crossed the massive parking lot, the Mexican reached for his cell phone. Robel knew enough Spanish at this point to recognize that he was talking to his accomplices in the truck, not family members as the smuggler claimed.

Once in the megastore, Robel was told to fill up the shopping cart with sodas and any foods they would need while waiting for the Western Union correction and money to come through. They would also buy an international phone card. Robel did not have a single coin left to his name, but the English-speaking smuggler said he would pay for everything.

As Robel filled the cart, he kept one eye on the coyotaje, who talked rapidly and intensely on the cell phone, while moving further and further away from Robel, down the aisles.

Robel had the feeling that something wasn't right, and his ominous intuition was confirmed when the guy headed back towards the exit. That's when the African ran for it, leaving the shopping cart behind to chase down the coyotaje.

Right outside of the doors, Robel grabbed him by the shirt and yelled, "You can't leave me here!" A scuffle erupted between the two, and Robel pleaded with passersby to help him. Everyone just looked down or away, refusing to get involved.

All the stress, frustration, difficulties, and hardship had finally caught up with Robel, culminating in anger and panic. I asked Robel if he really expected the smugglers to say, "OK, sorry, we'll take you back."

He said no, he basically wasn't thinking at all. He was just determined not to let go of the Mexican and be abandoned. He'd grabbed the shoulder strap of the coyotaje's white tank top. It quickly twisted around his fist during the scuffle. Eventually it ripped, freeing the coyotaje, and they both took off towards the truck.

The other two smugglers saw the fight and were waiting with a gun. When Robel saw it pointed at him, he turned and left.

In hindsight, he figured everything out: They'd cashed the money ($5,000 that was supposed to cover both Robel and his friend's passage) and were going to report that *he'd* cashed it and ran. Since they didn't kill him and dump his body, he would never be discovered. He would certainly not return. How could he? He didn't know where he was. The three smugglers would also still be able to charge his friend for his fee. Their bosses would never know what really happened and, with no witnesses, they were free to repeat the runner scenario at some point in the future.

Fortunately, the Eritrean (who was picked up earlier by a relative) had given out his Houston telephone number to *everyone* in his group, before leaving the house. Robel had slipped it into his pants pocket as well.

"Did you have to steal a phone, since you had no money at all?" I asked him.

> No, I found a black homeless man and ask him please help me. The American gave me a quarter and dialed number for me. He very nice.

Location: Oakland, California
Interview: 9:46 a.m., August 30, 2013, Peet's Coffee, Mill Valley, CA

Robel didn't have enough command of the English language to freely converse with the woman who answered the phone, so the homeless man took over. The newly arrived Eritrean wasn't there. The husband was at work. She didn't drive. She had to talk to her neighbor to see if he could give Robel a ride.

> Where am I? I don't know. Homeless guy say her where they are at, shopping center where Walmart is, and asked her where she at. He say me it's about 30 minutes away.

> After 1–½ hours neighbor arrive. He'd also brought Eritrean with him. We go to his house. Eat lunch. Shower. "Lucky they don't take your live. A lot of violence." He buy me clothes. Pajama. I sleep two, three hours. His kids came home from school.

> They so nice. They even speak my language: Tigrina.

> His wife come from work. We drink coffee, then all of us going neighbor's house. How was it? How was problem? When we chatting, we get phone call [Robel snaps his fingers]. It's around 11 at night. It's from two Eritrean men and womans from same group.

> The coyotajes say them: Robel took money and run away. Robel supposed pay for your friend. Friend have pay $300 extra because Robel run. They took all four Eritreans out, dumped them way out. They see some guy walking around and asked, "Can you help us please?" Guy gets on pay phone and explains where they are.

The Houston family, my friend's family, was nervous helping them. Maybe Mexicans are waiting and going kidnap them too? When they come for Eritreans. He don't have choice, so he got neighbor guy, and they have take risk. Then they went there. Two Eritrean ladies have family members in Houston. They came first. So they called and say us, never mind, we have a ride now.

Robel's friend's Houston family, plus the neighbor, turned back. That night, Robel slept at the neighbor's home because they had a spare room, and his Eritrean friend slept at his family's home.

Out of the four remaining refugees, two men wanted to go to D.C. Two women plus Robel wanted to come to California.

There's a company that driving people all over the USA. They take van, car, whatever, plus driver. It was $700, each person. Taking four days. We drove drove, drove, drop. Stop for eating food like McDonald's. Driver get tired. Asked if anyone else drive? I drove for 50 or 60 miles. It safer than [Robel makes a swerving steering wheel sign] driver. The driver called ahead and drop people in L.A., Santa Monica, San Jose. Last stop Oakland: two ladies and me.

Robel tilted his cup, finished off the last bit of coffee, and smiled.

EPILOGUE

WELCOME LOVE
Location: Novato, California
Interview: 12:00 p.m., May 10, 2013, Sandkuhler Studio,
Tiburon, California

During *his* time in Rome, Yodit and Robel corresponded via
Yahoo Messenger at Internet café's. During *my* time, sitting at
our local Starbucks in Strawberry Village with Robel, taking
notes, I occasionally see him responding to an incoming text
from "Love." His past and present merge now as this book is
being written. It should be no surprise when I reveal to you
that he was able to bring his love to join him in the United
States.

The first time I saw Yodit was when (dressed up and layered
in beautiful white and traditional clothing, gold jewelry,
intricately coiffed hair that peeked out of her *netsela*), she was
led in by others of her community amongst trills and gaiety. It
was her welcoming party, held at a humbly decorated church
dining room in Novato, California. Posters of Yodit and Robel's
wedding adorned the walls along with homemade, Eritrean
pride posters. The rich smells of a feast filled the air.

I imagined her freshly jet lagged from having flown in from a
foreign land. Her passage had taken her from Sudan to
Ethiopia, where she spent two months living with family while
getting processed by the U.S. Embassy. From there, she flew
through Germany and then into San Francisco.

Her face was open but not smiling as her entourage escorted
her, in measured steps, to be seated at the head table. Robel
was beaming, as the rest of us were beaming for them.
Traditional food had been made well in advance and was
being kept hot by sterno in their metal trays.

After the initial elation died down, we formed a line to load up
our plates. Everyone ate with their hands, using the spongy

140

bread to sop up rich stews made of locally farm-raised goat, lamb, and beef. Relatives and friends took turns approaching the head table and individually welcoming her. Those closest to Yodit and Robel shared the intimate ritual of *Gursha*: gently using one's hand to place food directly into another's mouth, while simultaneously touching them. A proverb from this part of the world states, "Those who eat from the same plate will not betray each other."

Several older women arrived. As an outsider, they appeared to be wise grandmothers to me: regally dressed and nearly completely covered, in layered white embroidered cotton *jellebyas*. Their heads were lightly covered in thin shawls.

The rest of the afternoon was filled with loud music and a slow, circular type of dancing called *quda*. Feet shuffling to the beat of the music, everyone bobbed their shoulders. The circle grew as more and more family and friends joined in. Occasionally, women trilled to signify great joy. The rhythmic head and neck movements of some of the men had a playful, congenial, and competitive undertone of who could be the most suave, while remaining deliberately understated. Everyone seemed to take a turn, which was usually followed up by good-natured laughter.

Two and three people took turns breaking off and dancing in the middle of the ever-turning circle, facing each other for a short time. The beats increased, and the pace stepped up. The more nimble of dancers jumped and went low to the floor while continuing to bob their shoulders to the beat. Eventually, the whole dance collapsed into a crescendo of laughter— marking the end.

I wish I could have spoken directly to Yodit to tell her how happy I was to finally meet her. Instead, I hung back and got to know Robel's Latino neighbors from his apartment building with whom we were sharing a table.

ACKNOWLEDGEMENTS

A very special thanks to the following people who helped shape this book: Mark Hogsett for the first read through and encouragement. Amy Rose, for (as you put it) your hyper grammatical vigilance. Tammy Sneider for lively discussions, pointed questions and suggestions for a study guide and interview. Dale and Lauren Engelbert for another round of (oh so polite) grammatical "suggestions" that helped tighten up the story. I really appreciated all y'alls help.

A belated gratitude to Royce Osborn who provided the initial spark (in the 1980's) that led to my interest in literature and cultures boarding the Sahara. I wish I'd gotten this to you in time.

ABOUT THE AUTHORS

IRIS SANDKÜHLER

In contrast to the challenging journey the main character faced, Iris Sandkühler immigrated to the United States in 1965, at the age of seven, with her German mother, who was a war bride. A year after she arrived, she became an avid journal keeper. This practice has continued throughout her life.

GHIRMAY NEGHASI

In May of 2000, Ghirmay Neghasi was taken out of school and forced to participate in mandatory military training in Gahtelay, Eritrea. After serving, he returned to his school and village to work as a mechanic.

In 2003, he was, once again, forced to join the military. This time he was taken to Sawa Military Camp for his miltary training. From September 2003 to June 2004, he continued high school in Sawa, until he was assigned to a platoon, to work as a mechanic.

In 2006, his battalion was taken to Alighidir, Eritrea, to work on a privately owned farm, picking cotton and harvesting millet. The farm was owned by officers, not the government. When Ghirmay and his colleagues decided to strike and gather to pray, their living spaces were searched. A journal listing all the abuses was found, and Ghirmay, plus a friend, were taken to an underground cell in Haykota, Eritrea. There, he was interrogated and regularly beaten with a rubber club. He spent eight months in the underground cell living on nothing but bread and water.

In December 2006, approximately 50 of the prisoners were taken to a government-owned farm in Haykota. The human rights abuses continued. Ghirmay and two friends decided to escape. One was shot and fell as the soldiers fired on them in a field. They never heard from their friend again.

With the help of a nomadic tribe, the two escaped soldiers made it to Khartoum, Sudan. There, Ghirmay joined the Eritrean Democratic Party to help bring about reform.

> While I was in Khartoum, I learned about a businessman who was arranging travels to the United States of America for payment. In March of 2007, I traveled from Sudan to Nairobi, Kenya, by plane with a false Ethiopian passport. After two weeks in Nairobi, I traveled by plane and entered Mexico City. From there, I traveled to Reynosa, Mexico, by bus. After two days in Reynosa, I crossing a river at the border and entered the USA in 2007, through McAllen, Texas, without inspection.
>
> After I left my country, the government went to my home looking for me. They arrested and detained my parents for two weeks in order to bring me back into the government's custody. They released them after they made a payment of 50,000 Nakfa, which is about $2,500.

At the time of this writing, Ghirmay continues to support the democratization of Eritrea. You may run into him working one of his many jobs that he juggles to support his immediate and extended family: a stock clerk at Whole Foods, night janitor at Marin General Hospital, rental property manager, or barista at Starbucks.

Made in the USA
Las Vegas, NV
24 December 2021